A Tale of

Suddenly, a new age had begun; and in this great new Revolutionary Age, the days flew by as though in a wild dream. It was a dream of blood and terror.

It is the end of the eighteenth century and Revolution shakes France and all of Europe. As the French people rise against the evil of their rulers, no one knows where their anger will end. No one can be sure they are safe.

Not even good citizen Doctor Manette, his daughter Lucie and the mysterious man she marries. Not a steady businessman, like Jarvis Lorry, or less honest men, like John Barsad. And not Sydney Carton, for whom the Revolution may be his one and only chance to make his life worthwhile.

Charles Dickens's great historical novel paints a powerful picture of the French Revolution and the lives of its unforgettable characters.

Charles Dickens (1812–70) is one of the greatest and best-loved of all British novelists. He was born in Portsmouth, England, but grew up in London and Chatham. His parents were very poor, mainly because of his father's inability to control money. At one time, the whole family was in prison because of the father's debts.

As a result, Dickens was sent to work in a factory at the age of twelve and had little formal education. Much of his childhood was a time of great unhappiness which stayed with him all his life. It left him with a fear of poverty but also a great sympathy for the poor. He worked hard at everything he did, first teaching himself enough to work as a journalist, then, in his early twenties, writing his first stories and novels.

These made him one of the most popular novelists in Victorian Britain – but he never stopped work, and his many books became famous all over the world. He died at the age of fifty-eight and was buried in Westminster Abbey. Thousands of people went to see him and drop flowers into his grave. Among them were found bunches of small, ordinary flowers dropped by the poor.

A Tale of Two Cities

CHARLES DICKENS

Level 6

Retold by David Wharry
Series Editors: Andy Hopkins and Jocelyn Potter

Addison Wesley Longman Limited
Edinburgh Gate, Harlow,
Essex CM20 2JE, England
and Associated Companies throughout the world.

ISBN 0 582 40278 6

A Tale of Two Cities was first published in 1859
This adaptation first published by Penguin Books 1991
This edition first published 1998

Text copyright © David Wharry 1991
Illustrations copyright © David Cuzik 1991
All rights reserved

The moral right of the adapter and of the illustrator has been asserted

Designed by D W Design Partnership Ltd
Set in 11/14pt Lasercomp Bembo
Printed in Spain by Mateu Cromo, S.A. Pinto (Madrid)

Published by Addison Wesley Longman Limited in association with
Penguin Books Ltd., both companies being subsidiaries of Pearson Plc

Dictionary words:

● As you read this book, you will find that some words are in darker black ink than the others on the page. Look them up in your dictionary, if you do not already know them, or try to guess the meaning of the words first, and then look them up later, to check.

On a foggy Friday night in late November 1775, Mr Jarvis Lorry walked up Shooter's Hill beside the Dover mail coach.

CHAPTER ONE

The Mail

On a foggy Friday night in late November 1775, Mr Jarvis Lorry walked up Shooter's Hill beside the Dover mail **coach**. The fog was so thick he could not even see the horses, only hear the driver's whip as they struggled up the long slope. Beside him, the other two passengers walked silently on in their muddy boots and heavy coats, their collars turned up around their ears.

Everyone was afraid. The guard riding behind the coach, a hand on one of six loaded guns, suspected the passengers as much as the darkness around him. The passengers suspected one another, the coachman, the guard. Everyone suspected everybody else of being a robber.

'Wo-ho!' cried the coachman. 'One more pull now!' And one final effort dragged the coach to the top.

As the guard was getting down to open the door for the passengers, the coachman cried, 'Tsst! Joe!'

'What do you hear Tom?'

Everyone listened, their hearts beating almost loud enough to be heard.

'A horse coming,' whispered the guard. 'Someone riding fast.' He climbed quickly up to his place and grabbed a gun.

The sound of the horse came closer, quickly.

'You there!' the guard cried out. 'Stop, or I shall fire!' They heard the horse stop, and a man's voice call from the fog, 'Is that the Dover mail?'

'Never you mind what it is!' shouted the guard. 'Who are you?'

'If it is the Dover mail I want to see a passenger, Mr Jarvis Lorry.'

'I am he, and I know this messenger,' Mr Lorry said to the guard immediately. 'Is that you, Jerry?' he shouted.

'Yes, sir. I have a message for you. From Tellson's Bank.'

A horse and rider came out of the fog.

'If you have a gun, keep your hand away from it!' warned the guard.

The rider handed Mr Lorry a small piece of paper. He opened it in the light of the coach lamp and read it – first to himself, then aloud: '"Wait at Dover for Mademoiselle."' He thought for a moment, then said, 'Jerry say that my answer is, RECALLED TO LIFE.'

'Recalled to life,' repeated Jerry. 'That's a strange answer, sir.'

'Take that message back to Tellson's, Jerry. Go now. Good night.'

Mr Lorry climbed into the coach where the other two passengers, their watches and money hidden in their boots, were pretending to be asleep.

Jerry Cruncher rode back to London, stopping in beer-houses along the way, while Mr Lorry travelled on along the road to Dover. As the banker sat half-asleep watching the night shadows rush past outside the coach window, the same thought came back to him again and again: 'Eighteen years! To be buried alive for eighteen years!'

CHAPTER TWO

The Preparation

The next morning, Mr Lorry was the only passenger to get out of the damp and dirty coach when it arrived at the Royal George Hotel in Dover. The other two had got out at different destinations along the way.

Wrapped from head to foot in his muddy travelling clothes, he was shown to his room and told there would be a boat to Calais the next day. Later, he came downstairs for breakfast in a plain, well-kept brown suit.

Mr Lorry listened to the sound of his pocket watch as he sat **staring** into the dining-room fire. He was a quiet, neat, stiff-looking gentleman of sixty. His plain, uninteresting face was as it nearly always was – empty of expression. When breakfast arrived he asked for a room to be prepared for a young lady who would be arriving from London.

In the afternoon, he went for a walk along the windy sea shore. The air was clear enough to see the French coast. After dinner, as he was pouring his last glass of wine, he heard the sound of wheels outside. A few minutes later, he was told that Miss Manette had arrived and would be happy to see him. Mr Lorry adjusted his odd little **wig** and followed the waiter to her room.

A golden-haired girl of not more than seventeen stood waiting for him by the fire, her hat still in her hand. Her blue eyes met his in the candlelight and, for one moment, Mr Lorry remembered a child he had held in his arms on a journey across the Channel, many years ago.

'Please take a seat, sir,' Lucie Manette said in a clear and pleasant young voice, with a slight foreign accent. Mr Lorry kissed her hand and sat down.

'I received a letter from the bank, sir, telling me there had been a discovery concerning the property of my poor dead father.' Mr Lorry moved uncomfortably in his chair. 'I was told to go to Paris and meet a man from the bank there. He would explain the details.'

'That man is me. Yes, I . . .' He paused. 'It is very difficult to begin, miss.'

Thoughtfully, she raised her eyes to his. 'Are you *really* a stranger to me sir? I have a feeling . . .'

'Miss Manette, I am a businessman . . . I have no time for feelings. Please, think of me only as a . . . talking machine – truly, I am not much else.'

'Please tell me then, sir.'

'Miss, there has been no new discovery of money or property – Doctor Manette left all he owned in my care at

Tellson's. As you know, we have managed it for you ever since he – and then your mother died.'

'It was *you* who brought me to England!' she cried, taking him by the wrists.

'It was I, miss. I was managing Tellson's Bank in Paris at the time.'

'Please tell me what has been discovered, sir!'

'Miss Manette, your father has been – been found. He is alive. I am afraid he is greatly changed, almost a wreck. He has been taken to the house of his old servant in Paris, and we are going there – I, to recognize him; you, to bring him back to life.'

Lucie Manette spoke slowly, clearly, as though talking in a dream: 'I am going to see his ghost! It will be his ghost – not him!'

Suddenly, a fierce-looking, red-haired, red-faced woman wearing a hat like a huge cheese burst into the room. With one great push of her huge hand she sent Mr Lorry flying against the wall.

'You in brown! Couldn't you tell her what you had to tell her without frightening her to death! Do you call *that* being a banker!'

Recovering, Mr Lorry looked on as Lucie's servant placed the young woman's head on her shoulder. 'I hope, madame –'

'Miss! Miss Pross.'

'I hope, Miss Pross, that you will be accompanying Miss Manette to France.'

'Sir, if I was intended to go across salt water, would I have been born on an island!'

This was a difficult question to answer, and Mr Lorry went downstairs to think about it.

CHAPTER THREE

The Wine Shop

A large **barrel** of wine had fallen out of a cart and broken in the street outside the wine shop. People dressed in rags had run to it and were drinking from little pools between the stones. The wine, mixed with dirt, ran like blood through their fingers. But the wine was soon gone, and the laughter stopped. Hollow-eyed, broken by sickness and hunger, the people walked slowly away; and the street in Saint Antoine, a poor suburb of Paris, became normal again.

Monsieur Defarge, the owner of the wine shop, had been in the street when the barrel had broken. 'Poor animals!' he had thought sadly, 'Most of them know only the taste of black bread and death.'

Ernest Defarge, a strong, dark-haired man of thirty, went into the wine shop. As always, Madame Defarge was sitting knitting behind the counter. She was about her husband's age, with a strong, hard face. Her cold dark eyes never seemed to look at anything in particular, but nothing escaped their attention.

'The people from the market broke a barrel,' said Defarge.

'It is not our affair. Let them bring another,' she said expressionlessly, putting down her knitting. She coughed, deliberately, signalling to him with her eyes – towards Mr Lorry and Lucie Manette, sitting in the corner.

'It must be them,' Defarge said quietly. Three friends of his were playing cards at a table next to the well-dressed couple. He went over to the three men.

'Good day, Jacques,' he said to the first.

'A fine day, Jacques,' the man replied without smiling.

'Hello, Jacques,' Defarge said to the second man.

'How goes it, Jacques,' he answered.

'Jacques,' Defarge said to the third friend. 'The room you

were asking about is on the fifth floor. You may go and visit it without me, if you like.'

The man looked at Lucie and Mr Lorry, then at the others. 'Thank you, Jacques,' he said to Defarge, and all three got up.

As they were leaving Mr Lorry tapped Defarge gently on the shoulder, 'Sir, could I have a few words with you?'

CHAPTER FOUR

The Shoemaker

Defarge led Mr Lorry and Lucie Manette up dark and dirty stairs behind the wine shop. It got steeper and narrower the higher they went and Mr Lorry stopped twice to rest. The smell of the rubbish everywhere made Lucie feel sick. When they turned the last corner they saw Defarge's friends by a door at the top of the stairs. They were looking at something through a tiny hole in the wall.

'Leave us, my friends,' Defarge shouted. 'We have business here.'

They came quietly down, saying nothing as they passed.

'Who are these men?' asked Mr Lorry.

'They are – of the chosen few.' There was a wild, secret look in Defarge's eyes when he said the last words. He took a key from his pocket.

'Is the door locked, sir?' asked Mr Lorry, surprised.

'He has lived so long locked up,' Defarge replied. 'He would be frightened – who knows what might happen if his door was left open.'

Lucie's face showed such an expression of anxiety, Mr Lorry took her by the hand – she was trembling with terror.

'Courage, miss. The worst part is now – before we open the door. Please, think of the good, the happiness you bring him. Open now, Defarge.'

Defarge turned the key in the lock and slowly opened the door. 'You may go in,' he said quietly.

'I am afraid,' said Lucie, shaking now.

'Of what?' asked Mr Lorry.

'Of him. Of my father.'

'Come now! We must go in!' said Mr Lorry with unusual impatience, a tear shining on his cheek.

Inside, the light was so dim it was difficult to see anything at all. Yet work was being done in there. With his back to them, facing a crack of light from the window, a white-haired old man sat on a low bench making shoes.

'You are still at work, I see,' said Defarge, looking down at the thin figure.

After a long silence, the head raised slightly and a voice spoke, as if from a distance. 'Yes – I am working.' The voice was like the last faint echo of a sound made long ago. A pair of lifeless eyes looked up at the questioner a moment before the face dropped again.

They stood watching the shoemaker for several minutes before Defarge opened the window to let in more light. He stopped working, an unfinished shoe visible now on his lap. He had a hollow face with extremely bright eyes that seemed to shine. His ragged shirt hung loosely around his worn, wasted body. Confused, he raised a hand to shade his eyes from the light.

'You have a visitor,' said Defarge. The shoemaker looked at him blankly as before. 'Tell monsieur what kind of shoe you are working on.'

'It is a lady's shoe,' said the old man mechanically.

'Now,' said Defarge, 'Tell monsieur the name of its maker.'

'One Hundred and Five, North Tower,' was the reply. Then, with a sigh, he began working again, ignoring his visitors.

'Monsieur Manette,' said Mr Lorry, laying a hand on his shoulder. 'Don't you recognize me?' There was no reply.

Tears running down her face, Lucie walked up to him.

The old man's eyes caught sight of her dress and he raised them. When he saw her face he stared at her with sudden fear and confusion. After a while, his lips began to form words, though no sound was heard.

Lucie sat down on the bench beside him and took his hands. He stared at her golden hair, at her hands holding his.

'Is it you?' he whispered. 'No. No, it cannot be. You cannot be my wife. You are too young.'

'Father! Father!' cried Lucie. She went down on her knees in front of him, threw her arms around him, pressed his wasted body to hers.

'You are the jailer's daughter?'

'Father, your pain is over! I have come to take you to peace and rest.'

'What is your name, gentle angel?' whispered the old man, tears appearing in his eyes.

CHAPTER FIVE

Five Years Later

Tellson's Bank in Fleet Street was an old-fashioned place, even in 1780. It was small, dark, and ugly. Curiously, however, its owners were proud of this. They believed that if it was any bigger, less dark, or less ugly, it would no longer be respectable.

It was Jerry Cruncher's job to wait outside Tellson's until he was called inside. Jerry was Tellson's messenger. It was Jerry's young son's job to sit beside his father.

Outside the bank on that windy March morning, young Jerry knew better than to talk to his father. Jerry had been out all night again and was in a very bad mood indeed. Jerry often went out all night and his son often wondered what he did. He certainly did not go fishing, as he pretended.

Jerry spat out the piece of grass he was chewing, wiped his hands across his mouth and scratched his untidy hair. His son looked up at him. They looked like each other – like a couple of monkeys.

The door opened and a voice shouted, 'Messenger!' Jerry murmured to himself and went inside.

'I want you to go to the Old Bailey law court,' said one of Tellson's oldest bankers. 'Give this letter to the door-keeper. He will give it to Mr Lorry.'

'Then what do I do, sir?'

'Remain there until he needs you. He is a witness. A customer of Tellson's has been accused of **treason**.'

'Treason! He will be hanged.'

'Yes – if he is found guilty. Go quickly now.'

Death is Nature's cure for many diseases, and in those days it was Justice's cure for nearly two hundred different crimes. The Old Bailey court was famous as a kind of inn that criminals visited briefly on their way from prison to the Other World.

Jerry began to sweat with fear as he approached the building. He rubbed his neck unconsciously. Smiling nervously, he handed the letter to the door-keeper. After a delay, he was allowed to go into the court.

Jerry pushed his way into the noisy crowd. Their breath smelled of beer and sausages. He could see Mr Lorry sitting at a table with gentlemen wearing wigs, next to the prisoner's lawyer. One of the gentlemen in wigs was sitting with his hands in his pockets, staring at the ceiling.

Jerry managed to catch Mr Lorry's attention. As the banker nodded in reply, a sudden murmur went round the court. Two jailers were bringing the prisoner in. Everybody turned to stare at him except the wigged gentleman with his hands in his pockets. He went on staring at the ceiling.

The prisoner was a good-looking man of about twenty-five, plainly dressed in a dark grey suit. His hair, which was long and dark, was gathered in a ribbon at the back of his neck. His naturally brown cheeks were pale as he bowed to the judge and stood quietly.

A mirror hanging above the prisoner reflected the impatient crowd. The sentence hanging over him was death. He knew he was already being mentally hanged by every person there, many of whom had paid to watch.

'Silence in the court!' shouted the judge.

CHAPTER SIX

A Disappointment

'Silence!' the judge repeated. 'The prisoner, Charles Darnay, is accused of being a **traitor** to His Majesty, King George. Coming and going regularly between France and our fine and royal kingdom, he has, on several occasions, delivered state secrets to the French.'

Every eye in the crowd watched Charles Darnay as he listened calmly to the judge. Then, when for some reason he looked to his left, every eye followed his to two figures, a young lady of little more than twenty, and a handsome white-haired gentleman who was obviously her father. She sat with her arm in his, staring with pity at the accused.

A whisper went about the court: 'Who are they?'

The Attorney-General★ stood up, bowed to judge and jury, and turned to question the accused.

'Mr Darnay, we have found that you have been in the habit of passing regularly between England and France on secret and evil business. This business might have remained undiscovered if Mr John Barsad, a fine and honest gentleman

★ An attorney-general is a lawyer, working for the state, whose job is to prove the accused is guilty.

– a friend of yours – had not searched your pockets and found secret papers.'

He turned confidently to the jury. 'I ask the jury to consider those papers as proof of his evil trade. I ask the jury – honest people, as I know they are – to find the prisoner guilty. Honest English people will never sleep safely unless his head is taken off.'

Mr Stryver, Darnay's lawyer, a heavy red-faced man, stood up. 'I wish to question the "fine and honest gentleman", John Barsad.' The wigged gentleman sitting next to Stryver went on staring at the ceiling.

A forty-year-old man, sweaty and very nervous, came to the witness-box. His nose looked as if it had once been broken: it was bent towards his left cheek.

'Have you ever been a spy, Mr Barsad?'

'No. I am a gentleman.'

'How many times have you been in prison for debt, sir? Four or five times, is it? I also believe you borrowed money from Mr Darnay and never paid him back.'

'That is not true, sir!'

'Your nose, Mr Barsad. Was it not broken when you were kicked down the stairs for cheating at cards?'

Stryver continued, ignoring the laughter. 'Mr Barsad, Mr Darnay tells me you are not a friend of his. He only met you a few times – once on a coach between London and Paris.' Stryver paused. His colleague continued to stare at the ceiling. 'Mr Barsad, the Attorney-General conveniently forgot to mention that the so-called "secret papers" were not written in Mr Darnay's handwriting. Did you not put them in Mr Darnay's pocket yourself – perhaps even write them yourself?'

'That's a lie!' shouted Barsad desperately. Stryver sat down.

The Attorney-General called his next witness, Mr Lorry.

'Mr Lorry, on a Friday night in November 1775, did you travel between London and Dover?'

'Yes.'

'Were there any other passengers?'

'Two. But they got off before Dover, in different places during the night.'

'Was the prisoner one of those passengers?'

'I cannot say. We were all so wrapped up in our clothes.'

'Mr Lorry, have you ever seen the prisoner before?'

'Yes. I was returning from France a few days afterwards and he came on the boat at Calais. I was travelling with two companions. The four of us finished the journey together.'

The next person he questioned was Lucie Manette.

'Miss Manette, you and your father were travelling with Mr Lorry. Did you talk to the prisoner on the journey?'

'Of course. He was a kind man and helped us in every way he could.'

'Did he say anything about America?'

'We talked about the trouble between England and America.'

'Be exact, Miss Manette.'

'He said that there were two sides to every quarrel, and that history would remember George Washington more than George III.' There was a sudden angry roar in the court.

'Did he come on the boat alone.'

'No, with two men, but they went back on shore again.'

'Were any papers handed among them?'

'I think so, yes.'

'Like these in shape and size?'

'It is impossible for me to say.'

He then called the young lady's father as witness.

'Doctor Manette, have you ever seen the accused before?'

'Yes, he came to our house in London about three years ago.'

'You have no memory of him on the journey from Calais to London?'

'No. My mind is blank. I cannot even say when I first remember my daughter. When my memory came back to me, I was already living in London.'

The Attorney-General went on to show that Darnay had got out of the coach near Dover on that night in November 1775. He went to a nearby harbour to spy on ships of the Royal Navy. He called a witness, Roger Cly, who said he saw Darnay there that night.

Mr Stryver was questioning Cly when his colleague at last looked down from the ceiling and wrote a few words on a piece of paper. He threw it to the lawyer who, after a thoughtful pause, asked Cly if he was quite sure it was Darnay he saw that night. Cly repeated that he was certain.

'Mr Cly, look carefully at Mr Carton here.' Cly's and the whole court's eyes went to the man looking at the ceiling. He looked down and took off his wig.

'Now, Mr Cly, look at the prisoner. Do not Mr Darnay and Mr Carton look alike?' Cly – and everybody in the court – was amazed by how alike the two men were.

Mr Stryver turned to the judge. 'My Lord, are we going to try Mr Carton for treason next?' He went on to show the jury how the evidence had been twisted by the Attorney-General. He showed that Cly was Barsad's friend and that they were both professional spies.

The jury went out to decide if Darnay was guilty or not. There was no doubt about this for most people in the court, and the decision was expected to come quickly.

As Mr Stryver gathered his papers, Mr Carton sat looking at the ceiling as he had all day. There was something unhealthy about this man. His untidy wig had been put on carelessly. Nothing seemed to interest him.

Yet, he noticed every detail of the scene. When Lucie Manette's head dropped onto her father's chest, he called an officer immediately.

'Officer, help the gentleman take the young lady out. Don't you see she feels faint.'

Mr Lorry accompanied the Manettes out of the court.

Mr Stryver was questioning Cly when Carton wrote a few words on a piece of paper. He then threw it to the lawyer.

A rumour spread that the jury could not agree. When Mr Lorry came back, Mr Carton asked after Miss Manette.

'She is still very disturbed indeed, but she feels better.'

'I will tell the prisoner.' He went over to Darnay.

'You will be glad to hear that Miss Manette is feeling better,' he said carelessly.

'Could you tell her that I am deeply sorry to have been the cause of her feeling ill.'

Carton laughed. 'Yes, if you want me to.'

'I do want you to. Thank you.'

The news sent a tide of people rushing out into the court.

'Jerry, Jerry!' shouted Mr Lorry. He handed Jerry a paper to take urgently to Tellson's. The message was two words: 'NOT GUILTY'.

Jerry, who could not read, said, 'What's the message, sir? "Recalled to life" again?'

CHAPTER SEVEN

Congratulations

In the dimly-lit passages, the last people were leaving the court. Doctor Manette, Lucie and Mr Lorry stood around Charles Darnay, congratulating him on his escape from death.

Darnay shook the Doctor's hand. Mr Lorry studied Manette's fine intellectual face as he spoke to Darnay in French. It was difficult to believe this was the face of the shoemaker in Paris. However, he knew that although Manette had recovered from his years of pain, dark moods still overcame him. Only Lucie had the power to lift these black clouds from his mind.

Mr Darnay kissed Lucie's hand. He then warmly thanked the big, loud, red-faced Mr Stryver who had just pushed his way into their company.

'I did my best for you, Mr Darnay, and my best is as good as any man's, I believe.'

He was obviously expecting someone to say, 'No, much better.' So Mr Lorry said it.

'Do you think so?' said the ambitious lawyer, smoothing his wig.

'Miss Lucie looks ill,' said Mr Lorry. 'And Mr Darnay has had a terrible day. We are all tired and should go home.'

'Speak for yourself, sir,' said Stryver. 'I still have a hard night's work in front of me.' He left them, pushing his way to the lawyer's room.

It was then that Mr Lorry noticed the way Doctor Manette was staring at Darnay. A strange expression − of distrust, mixed with fear − was frozen on his face.

They were already putting out the lights. Lucie took the Doctor by the arm. 'Father, shall we go home, now?'

But the old man did not hear her. His thoughts had wandered far away.

A figure, who had been standing by a wall in the shadows, followed them out into the street where a carriage was waiting for Lucie and the Doctor. They left immediately.

Next, it was the shy, business-like banker's turn to say goodbye. He could not stop himself from saying, 'God bless you sir! I wish you a happy life,' before getting into a carriage.

Darnay stood alone now in front of the great gates of the court, and Carton who had been waiting nearby, approached him. He smiled and slapped Darnay on the shoulder.

'This is a strange chance that throws you and me together.' He smelled of wine and appeared to be slightly drunk.

'I hardly feel I belong to this world again yet,' Darnay replied.

'I'm not at all surprised. A few minutes ago, you had one foot in the next world.'

'I feel a bit faint,' said Darnay.

'You need to eat,' Carton said. 'I will take you to supper.'

CHAPTER EIGHT

The Jackal

Carton took the Frenchman to an inn near Fleet Street, and Darnay was served food and wine immediately. Carton sat and watched him eat, drinking from a separate bottle of much stronger wine.

'It must be a wonderful feeling to return to this world after having almost left it,' said Carton with a strange, sour smile. '*My* greatest desire is to forget I belong to it. It has no good in it for me – except wine like this of course. Yes, I am beginning to think we are not at all alike, Mr Darnay.'

Seeing that Darnay did not know what to answer, Carton raised his glass suddenly. 'I drink to the good health of a beautiful lady.' Their eyes met. 'To Miss Manette!'

Darnay raised his glass slowly, searching Carton's eyes. 'To Miss Manette,' he said.

Carton emptied his glass and threw it over his shoulder. 'Yes,' he said. 'She was very pleased to receive your message when I gave it to her.' He laughed sarcastically.

'I thank you for that, Carton,' Darnay said, forcing himself to be polite. 'I also thank you for saving my life.'

'Hah! I want no thanks! I don't even know why I did it!' He drank another glass, filled it immediately, emptied it again. 'Tell me, Darnay,' he said. 'Do you think I like you?'

'I am beginning to think you don't.'

'I am beginning to think you are right. And I am sure you don't like *me*.'

Darnay got up angrily and rang a bell. 'Why do you drink so much, Carton?'

'Because I don't like myself. I care for no man! And no man cares for me!'

Darnay paid. 'You could have used your gifts much better, Carton,' he said, as he was leaving.

23

'Maybe yes, Mr Darnay, maybe no. Goodnight!'

Darnay was right. Carton had been a very good lawyer before he started drinking.

Alone, Carton studied himself in the mirror. 'You hate yourself,' he said, laughing at himself in the mirror. 'So why should you like a man who looks like you? Why? Because he shows you what you might have been?'

He drank the rest of his wine and fell asleep.

A waiter woke him at ten o'clock. He threw his coat on and walked out. After a short walk he reached Stryver's house and went inside.

'You are a little late, Carton,' Stryver said as Carton entered the untidy office full of books and papers, 'And already drunk, I see.' Stryver poured them both large drinks from one of the many bottles on the table.

Stryver was a successful and ambitious lawyer. He was also a heavy drinker like Carton. They drank together most nights, and always appeared together in court. They were known as 'the Lion and his **Jackal**.'

'That was a good idea of yours today, Carton,' said Stryver. 'Now, get to work.'

Carton put a towel into a jug of cold water, fixed the towel round his head. 'I am ready,' he said, sighing.

Stryver pointed at two enormous heaps of papers.

Carton began studying them silently, making notes. The Lion poured his Jackal another large drink and sat down to wait. Exhausted, the Jackal put the last paper down as the sun was coming up. He finished the notes for the day's two cases and left without waking the Lion.

CHAPTER NINE

Hundreds of People

On a fine Sunday afternoon, four months after the trial, Mr Lorry was on his way to have lunch with the Manettes. He had become a friend of the family and was often invited there.

Their apartment was in a quiet street near Soho Square. Mr Lorry felt at home there, and loved to sit in the echoing garden, listening to the birds and the distant sounds of the city.

There was no one there when Mr Lorry rang the bell. However, as he was expected, he decided to go inside. He went along the hall, past the Doctor's office. He received his patients there, for he was now working again. His scientific knowledge and great skill had already earned him a solid reputation.

He went into the sitting-room, admiring the colourful way Lucie had decorated it. The Doctor's bedroom door was open and he was surprised to see the shoemaker's bench and tools in the corner.

'I wonder why he keeps them,' Mr Lorry said to himself.

'And *why* do you wonder?' said a sharp voice that made him jump. It was Miss Pross, the fierce woman he had first met in Dover. Miss Pross's bark was worse than her bite – in fact, she had a heart of gold – and she made Mr Lorry laugh with her way of exaggerating everything.

'How are you, Miss Pross?'

'I am most worried about my dear **Ladybird**, Mr Lorry. Hundreds of unsuitable people keep visiting her all the time.'

'Oh dear,' was the safest thing Mr Lorry could think of replying. He knew her to be very jealous. She had taken care of Lucie since she was ten years old. In Miss Pross's eyes the only man suitable for Lucie was her younger brother, Solomon. Mr Lorry thought he had better change the subject.

'Does the Doctor ever talk about the shoemaking time?'

'Never.'

'Do you think he has a theory about who put him in prison?'

'I only think we had better leave those things alone, Mr Lorry. They are not good for our poor Doctor to think about. Sometimes he gets up in the middle of the night and walks up and down. My Ladybird gets up and walks with him until he is calm again.'

They heard footsteps. 'Ah, here they are!' said Miss Pross.

Mr Lorry was still expecting hundreds of people to arrive when Miss Pross served lunch. The air was hot and heavy, and after they had eaten Lucie suggested they should go out into the garden. They sat talking. Still no hundreds of people. Mr Darnay arrived, but he made only one. Miss Pross pretended to feel ill and went into the house. Once, as they talked, Mr Lorry noticed Doctor Manette staring at Darnay with that same strange expression he had seen in the corridor of the Old Bailey. Teatime came. Still no hundreds of people. Mr Carton had arrived, but that made only two.

It was a hot night and they sat with the doors and windows open. Rain began to fall in the heavy darkness. A wind blew dust across the garden.

'A storm is coming,' said Carton, listening to the echoes of hurrying footsteps in the street.

'Hundreds of people rushing home,' said Lucie.

'I can see a great crowd rushing towards us,' said Carton, a wild look in his eye. There was a flash of lightning. 'I can see them by the lightning. Here they come, fast and fierce!'

A huge storm broke, and didn't stop until after midnight. The great bell of Saint Paul's Cathedral struck one as Jerry Cruncher arrived to take Mr Lorry home.

'What a night it has been, Jerry,' said the banker as they left. 'A night to bring the dead out of their graves.'

Jerry gave him a very strange look indeed.

CHAPTER TEN

Monseigneur in Town

The Marquis* of Evrémonde's pale face was like a finely painted **mask**. It was a superior face, an extraordinary face, a face of great cruelty. Its owner, a luxuriously dressed man of about sixty, left the reception at the Tuileries Palace, got into his carriage, and drove away.

As always, his driver drove at breakneck speed through the narrow Paris streets. The mask smiled to itself as it watched the common people running away from the horses, some only just escaping being run over. Then, as they came round a corner by a fountain, the carriage wheels jumped as they ran over something. The carriage stopped and the driver got down, afraid one of his horses was hurt.

'What has gone wrong?' said the Marquis, calmly looking out.

A tall man in a night **cap** had taken a bundle of cloth from beneath the carriage and laid it by the fountain. He was kneeling in the mud, screaming.

'Pardon, Monseigneur†!' said another man. 'It is his child.'

'Killed!' screamed the man with the bundle. 'Dead!'

Silently, the crowd closed round the carriage. There was no expression in their faces, no visible sign of anger. The Marquis ran his eyes over them, as though they were rats that had come out of their holes to admire him.

'It is extraordinary to me that you people cannot take more care of yourselves. You are always getting in the way. You might have injured my horses.'

---

* Marquis is a rank of the French aristocracy.

† Monseigneur is the title given to French princes. The French common people used this word when they spoke to an aristocrat (the word in French means 'my lord').

'It is extraordinary to me that you people cannot take more care of yourselves. You are always getting in the way.'

He threw out a gold coin. All eyes looked down where it fell.

'Dead! Dead!' the father cried out again.

He was stopped by Defarge, who had just arrived. 'Be brave, Gaspard, be brave,' Defarge said. 'He died quickly, without pain. Could he have ever been as happy as he is now?'

People stepped back as Defarge came forward to the carriage.

'What is your name, Philosopher?' said the Marquis, smiling.

'I am Defarge, seller of wine.'

'Pick up that coin, Philosopher, seller of wine, and spend it as you please.'

The Marquis knocked on the ceiling and the carriage was moving away when the coin flew in through the window and rang on the floor.

'Hold the horses!' shouted Evrémonde. 'Who threw that?'

Madame Defarge pushed through the crowd to her husband. Defarge kneeled down beside the father and his dead bundle. The crowd stared at the Marquis in silence, afraid. They had long experience of what a man like this could do to them if he wanted. Only Madame Defarge dared to look the **aristocrat** in the face. Her eyes never left his pale mask as she stood there knitting. His eyes met hers.

'You dogs! I would ride over you all willingly!' he shouted, laughing. 'Driver! Go on!'

CHAPTER ELEVEN

Monseigneur in the Country

The last light of the evening sun shone brilliantly into Monseigneur's carriage as it reached the top of the hill. His powdered face was almost the colour of flesh in the blood-red light.

Evrémonde saw the roofs and towers of his great château* in the valley below. All around, the land belonged to him, in every direction, many times further than the eye could see. Once, corn had grown high in the fields. Now there were only small areas of poor beans and peas here and there.

They rode through the village, past people washing their food – anything that could be eaten. Their faces dropped as the carriage passed. Monseigneur ordered the driver to stop in the village square.

'Gabelle!' shouted the Marquis.

The village tax-collector approached and bowed to his master. Evrémonde pointed at the village road-mender.

'Bring him to me!'

Gabelle went over to him, took the man by the arm and brought him to the carriage. People closed around to listen.

'I passed you on the road,' said Evrémonde. 'What were you staring at?'

'Monseigneur, I was looking at the man.'

'The man?'

'Yes, Monseigneur, the man.'

'The man, the man? What man, you rat?'

'He was hanging under the carriage, Monseigneur. He was all covered with dust, whiter than a ghost.'

Everyone looked under the carriage. There was no man.

'Monseigneur, I saw him. He jumped off before the village.'

* A château is a very large house, palace or castle in the French countryside.

'You did well, dog. A thief, perhaps . . . Catch him if he enters the village tonight.'

The carriage drove away fast in a cloud of dust. Not far from the château, it slowed down on a short slope. In the half-darkness, Evrémonde noticed a woman kneeling by a small wooden cross.

'You! What are you doing?' he shouted. The woman came to him, crying. She looked old, but she was no more than twenty.

'There lies my son, Monseigneur. He died of hunger.'

'Well? Could I have fed him?'

'Monseigneur, so many more will die like him. Please, have pity on us!'

'Pity! One more or less of you animals – what do I care.'

The driver pushed the woman to one side and drove away.

Sweet smells rose in the moonlight as the Marquis drove through the beautiful gardens of his château. He got out in the soft shadow of one of the high towers and went up the curved staircase into the great mass of stone.

A servant carrying a torch walked in front of Monseigneur along dark corridors to a round room in one of the towers. A table was laid for two.

Monseigneur sat down to eat alone by the open window. As he was finishing his soup, he thought he heard something in the heavy darkness outside.

'What was that?' he said.

'It is nothing, Monseigneur,' said the servant, looking out. 'The trees and the night are all that are out there.'

Minutes later, a carriage drove into the gardens of the château.

'Tell my nephew supper is waiting for him,' said Monseigneur.

CHAPTER TWELVE

A Message from Jacques

The Marquis received Charles Darnay politely but they did not shake hands.

'I expected you to come much sooner,' he said with a smile.

'I was delayed by some unexpected business,' Darnay said, looking at his uncle with deep distrust. 'Dangerous business.'

'Without doubt,' replied Evrémonde after a pause.

'Nevertheless, death in England would have been better than prison here.'

The fine lines of Evrémonde's face grew longer. 'Death?' he said, almost sleepily. 'Please explain, my dear Charles.'

'Certain people were working together to prove I did something I did not do. Are *you* one of them?'

'No, no, no,' said the Marquis, smiling sweetly.

'Here in France, however, a simple letter written by you could send me to prison for ever.'

'It is possible,' said his uncle with great calmness.

'Uncle, you know why I have returned. I have come to try to persuade you –'

'Yet you know it is useless. You are a fool.'

Darnay could no longer control himself. 'We must change our ways! We have done wrong, uncle! Our family lives on the fruits of wrong. The name of Evrémonde is one of the most hated in France. It is a symbol of cruelty, suffering, starvation.'

'I am *proud* that people fear our great name, my dear Charles. And *I* shall see that they continue to.'

'If ever this land becomes mine, I shall free these people from the weight that drags them down.'

'The whip is the only thing that is good for these dogs. Yes, the whip is the only true philosophy.' He pointed a finger at Darnay's chest, like a sword. 'And like you, many who are afraid of that truth have run away – to England.' A faint smile appeared on Evrémonde's thin lips. 'A certain doctor, and his daughter, for instance.' The mask turned to stone again. 'You look tired, nephew. Goodnight.' He left the room.

It was a hot night. The Marquis walked up and down in his bedroom for a long time. It was two o'clock before he finally felt ready to sleep.

For four hours, the thick stone walls stared blindly at the night. Darkness, stillness lay on all things. Then, slowly, the dawn came. The birds were singing as the first sunlight entered the Marquis's bedroom window. Soon, the sun shone directly on the fine mask of his face.

There was a piece of paper on the Marquis's chest. A knife had been driven through the paper into the Marquis's heart. On the paper was written:

'Drive him fast to his grave. From Jacques.'

CHAPTER THIRTEEN

Two Promises

Twelve months had come and gone, and Charles Darnay was working as a French teacher in England. He divided his time between Cambridge, where he had found work at the University, and London.

In England, he had expected neither to walk on pavements of gold, nor to lie on beds of roses; he had expected to work. He worked hard and was beginning to do well for himself.

He had loved Lucie Manette ever since his escape from death at the treason trial. He had never seen a face so beautiful as hers when she stared pityingly at him across the Old Bailey courtroom. But, although he visited her regularly, he had not yet told her what he felt.

One summer day, late in the afternoon, Charles went to the

Manettes' house. He knew Lucie to be out with Miss Pross.

He found the Doctor studying in his chair by the window. He had now fully recovered from his prison years, and Charles admired the old man's energy and sharpness of mind.

'Charles!' he said, holding out his hand, 'I am so happy to see you. We were talking about you yesterday. Mr Carton and Mr Stryver came to visit Lucie. She is out, I'm afraid.'

'I know, Doctor. It was you I came to speak to.'

There was a silence.

'Is Lucie the subject?' said the Doctor.

There was another silence.

'Yes. Shall I go on, sir?'

Yet another silence.

'Yes, go on.'

'Sir, I love your daughter more than anything in the world.'

'I do not doubt that,' the Doctor said, without looking at Darnay. 'Have you told her?'

'No, sir.'

'Have you any reason to believe she loves you?'

'None, as yet, sir, none.'

'Is the object of your visit to find this out from me?'

'Not exactly, sir. Sir, if ever she were to tell you that she held me in her heart, could you mention what I have just said . . . that my feelings for her . . .'

'I see no reason for not doing so.'

'Thank you, sir. And if, one day, I had the possibility of asking for her hand in marriage . . .'

'Young man, I know your feelings to be pure and true. I promise I would not prevent you – if she loved you.'

Darnay took the Doctor's hand gratefully. Their hands still joined, the Doctor said, 'She is everything to me, as you know.'

'Sir, I want to return your confidence in me by telling you something about myself. Darnay is not my real name. My name –'

'Stop!' cried the Doctor, putting his hands to his ears.

'I do not want to keep this secret from you, sir! We have both run away from the evils of France –'

'No, I said!' The Doctor put his hand over Darnay's lips. 'If Lucie loves you, and you get married, then tell me on your marriage morning. Do you promise?'

'I promise, sir.'

It was dark when Charles Darnay left, and an hour later and darker, when Lucie came home. As she entered she heard hammering in her father's bedroom. She ran to him and gently took the shoemaker's tools away from him. They walked up and down together for a long time.

CHAPTER FOURTEEN

A Delicate Matter

'Sydney,' said Stryver to his Jackal, later that same night. 'I am going to tell you something that will rather surprise you.'

Carton had been working extra hard all night – it was already almost morning. Extra wine and wet towels had been necessary, and he was now in very poor condition.

'I am going to get married,' Stryver said from the sofa where he lay on his back.

Carton looked up from his work. 'Really?'

'Yes, and not for money.'

'Do I know the poor woman?'

'Guess'

Carton drank a glass of wine. 'I am not going to guess at five o'clock in the morning with my brains frying in my head.'

'Really, you are such an unpleasant person, Sydney.'

Carton laughed and drank more.

'Yes, you do know the "poor" woman. She is a delicate, golden-haired beauty called Miss Manette.'

Carton coughed, spilling drink on the papers. He began roaring with laughter.

'Are you surprised?' Stryver inquired very seriously.

Carton controlled his laughter. 'Why should I be?'

'I am already quite a rich man, Sydney. She is lucky to have me. Do you approve?'

'Why shouldn't I approve?' said Carton, with a sweet smile. 'It was most kind of you to think of her. To Miss Manette!' He emptied his glass and poured another immediately.

Stryver straightened his jacket over his generous stomach. 'Sydney, you are ruining yourself, you know. You'll wake up one day and find yourself alone, ill and poor. You really ought to think about a woman.'

'I do,' Carton replied, looking out at the grey dawn. 'And so, when are you going to tell the delicate flower about her good fortune?'

'I haven't made up my mind.'

CHAPTER FIFTEEN

The Secret

Sydney Carton had been coming often to visit the Manettes for over a year. He never shone in their company. When he felt like talking, he talked well, but the dark cloud of hopelessness and depression was always there, hanging over him. He gave the impression of caring for nothing.

When wine was no help to him, he wandered the streets at night. Sometimes, like a homeless ghost, he could be seen standing outside the house near Soho-square.

One fine day in August, he was out wandering, going nowhere, when he came to a decision. He began to walk faster and soon he arrived at the Manettes' house.

He was shown upstairs and found Lucie at her work, alone.

She had never felt comfortable with him and was embarrassed by his unexpected visit.

'Are you ill, Mr Carton?' she asked, concerned by his ghostly appearance.

'Miss Manette, the life I lead is not good for health.'

'Please excuse me for saying so, but isn't that a pity?'

'I am ashamed, yes.'

'Then why not change your life?'

There were tears in his eyes as he answered, 'It is too late. I shall never be better. I shall only sink lower.'

He covered his eyes and his body shook in silence. Lucie felt a wave of pity for him. Eventually, he uncovered his eyes and spoke.

'I beg you to excuse me. Miss Manette, there is something I want to say to you. Will you listen?'

Trembling, she said, 'Yes, if it makes you feel any happier.'

'I know you will never return the love of this wasted man you see before you. I simply wish you to know, Miss Manette, that you have been the last dream of my dying soul.'

'Mr Carton, I will always be your friend. I know there is good in you. I know you can begin again.'

'No. I am fast reaching my end.' He put her hand to his lips. 'Thank you for your concern.'

As he moved towards the door, Lucie began to cry.

'I am not worth your tears,' he said gently, turning to her again. 'Miss Manette, there is one last thing I will say. You must believe me when I say it, and it must remain a secret between us.'

Her eyes met his.

'I would give my life to save you, or anyone who is dear to you,' he said. He bowed and left her.

CHAPTER SIXTEEN

The Fisherman

Jeremiah Cruncher sat on his little chair outside Tellson's, cleaning rust from his fingernails. Young Jeremiah sat with him, a piece of grass in his mouth. Like two lazy fishermen, they watched the slow stream of traffic in Fleet Street.

The father was the first to notice a crowd of people in the distance.

'It appears to be a funeral procession, young Jerry,' he said, suddenly alert.

'Hooray, father!' cried young Jerry, giving his father a curious sideways look.

The procession approached. It was a strange procession for a funeral: people were dancing and shouting and crowding around the carriage that carried the **coffin**. Angry faces were shouting 'Yah! Spies! Tst! Yaha! Spies!'

'Who is it?' Jerry asked the first man who came past.

'A spy!' shouted the man, 'Spies! Yaha! Tst! Spies!'

He asked another man. 'Who is it.'

'Barsad. An Old Bailey spy. Spies! Yaha! Tst! Spies!'

Jerry suddenly remembered the trial. 'I've seen him. A healthy-looking man, he was. Dead, is he?'

'Dead as a door nail!' replied the man, laughing.

'A rusty door nail,' young Jerry said to himself with a secret smile.

The Bank closed, and the Crunchers went home. As they were passing the house of a famous doctor, Jerry suddenly complained of a pain in his liver.

'Jerry,' he said to his son, 'Go on home and tell your mother I'll be a little late for tea. Tell her I'm not feeling well and I've gone to the doctor.'

Later that night, Jerry was in an unusually good mood as he sat by the fire.

'Going out fishing tonight, are you?' Mrs Cruncher asked him.

'Yes, dear, I am.'

'Can I come with you, father?' said the youngest Cruncher.

'No you may not! It's time for you to go to bed now!'

After his son and his wife had gone to bed, Jerry sat smoking until nearly one o'clock. Then he took a key from his pocket and unlocked a cupboard. From it he took his fishing equipment: a sack, a chain, a thick iron bar and a rusty digging tool.

The next morning, there was no fish for breakfast, and Jeremiah Cruncher was in an extremely bad mood. His wife and son stayed a safe distance from him.

Like all children's minds, young Jerry's was full of questions, and on the way to the bank he asked his father, 'Father, what does a Resurrection-Man* do?'

His father stopped suddenly, and looked at his son extremely suspiciously.

'How should I know?'

'It's something to do with people's bodies, isn't it?'

Jerry Cruncher thought for a moment, 'Something like that, yes. It has something to do with medical science, I believe.'

'Father,' said the son.

'Yes, son,' said the father.

'I want to be a Resurrection-Man when I grow up.'

CHAPTER SEVENTEEN

Knitting

Madame Defarge had been knitting all the way from Saint Antoine. She was travelling to Versailles in a public carriage

---

* Resurrection – this is the idea that a dead person can come back to life. The act of coming back to life after death.

with her husband and three friends, Jacques Two, Jacques Three, and Jacques Four. They were going there to see the King and Queen.

'You work hard, madame,' said Jacques Two, grinning.

'Yes,' said Madame Defarge, 'I have a lot to do.'

'What are you knitting, madame?'

'Clothes for the dead.' A faint trace of a smile passed across her hard face.

Jacques Two laughed, and turned to Defarge. 'Are you sure this is a safe way to keep our records?' he whispered.

'Only she knows the secret meaning of the symbols in her knitting.'

'That is what I mean, she could forget.'

'Don't worry, even if my wife decided to keep the records in her head, she would not lose a single stitch.'

Later, as the crowd around them shouted 'Bravo! Bravo! Long live the King, long live the Queen!' the five from Saint Antoine watched in silence. They were not wishing long lives for the King and Queen in their golden coach, or for the laughing ladies and fine gentlemen in their jewels and silk and powder.

'Soon we will strip the feathers off those stupid decorative birds,' said Madame Defarge under her breath. 'Soon we will tear those pretty fools to pieces and eat them alive.'

'Not before a long time, I am afraid,' said her husband.

'Revenge always takes a long time,' she said, staring at the procession. 'It is a dish that is eaten cold.'

In the hot evening, they rode back to Paris. They got out at the barrier while their papers were examined, and Defarge saw a guard he knew.

'Jacques,' said the guard to Defarge, 'You must be careful. Another spy has been sent to Saint Antoine.'

'His name?' asked Madame Defarge.

'John Barsad. An Englishman.'

'What does he look like, Jacques?' asked the wine-seller.

'About forty, dark hair, thin; and his nose is not straight.'

'I shall record him tomorrow,' said Madame Defarge.

'You are a fine brave woman,' said the guard. 'We need more like you.'

'The Company of Jacques is growing stronger with every hour, my friend,' said Madame Defarge. 'The storm is gathering force.'

In the wine shop at noon the next day, the brave woman was sitting in her usual place when a figure entered. She took one look at the man and put down her knitting. Her eyes never leaving him, she took a rose from the counter and pinned it to her hat. This sudden decision to decorate herself had a strange effect: the customers stopped talking and, one by one, everyone left. Everyone, that is, except the new arrival. At the counter, he ordered a glass of wine. Madame Defarge served him and began knitting again.

'You knit with great skill, madame,' said Barsad. 'May I ask what it is you are making?'

'I do not know yet,' she said coldly. 'I may find a use for it one day.'

Ernest Defarge entered with two men. His companions turned and left as soon as they saw the rose.

'Here is my husband,' said Madame Defarge.

'Good day, Jacques,' said the spy with a friendly smile.

Defarge stopped and stared at him.

'Good day, Jacques,' Barsad repeated, less confidently.

'You have made a mistake, sir. My name is Ernest Defarge.'

'Never mind,' said the spy sweetly. 'Good day all the same.'

'Good day,' said Defarge coldly.

The spy emptied his little glass of wine. Madame Defarge filled it and began singing a little song softly to herself as she knitted.

'It is not often we see an Englishman in Saint Antoine,' said Defarge.

His wife gave him a quick sharp look. The message was: 'Watch what you say!'

'You know I am English?' said Barsad.

'By your accent, sir,' said Defarge awkwardly.

'You are right, of course, I am English, and it was in England that I first heard your name, Defarge.'

'Really?' the wine-seller said flatly.

'Yes, Defarge, I am well-informed of the circumstances of Doctor Manette's release from prison. His daughter and the neat brown banker took him from your care, did they not?'

'It is a fact,' said Defarge flatly.

'We received news of their safe arrival in London,' Madame Defarge said immediately. 'We have not heard from them since.'

'What a pity,' said Barsad. 'Then you will not know that Miss Manette is going to be married. To a Frenchman – the new Marquis of Evrémonde. He lives in England, under the name of Charles Darnay. His mother's family's name was d'Aulnais.'

Madame Defarge knitted steadily, recording everything, but her husband was visibly shocked when he heard the name d'Aulnais. His hand shook as he lit his pipe and the spy's trained eyes noticed this. His smooth voice went on, 'The previous Marquis of Evrémonde met with a very uncomfortable end, as I am sure you know. I believe his death was very much regretted by the people of Saint Antoine.'

'Yes,' said Madame Defarge, clearing her throat. 'We, and all France regretted the death of such a fine and noble man.'

Barsad bowed respectfully to her. 'I wish you good knitting, madame.' He paid and left.

For some minutes, the Defarges remained exactly as they were.

'If what he says is true,' said Defarge, 'And if the victory of the people –'

'Not *if*! *When*!' interrupted his wife.

'*When* our victory comes, I hope, for Miss Manette's sake, that her husband will not be in France.'

'Sympathy is for the weak!' said Madame Defarge. 'The

Madame Defarge knitted steadily, recording the conversation between her husband and Barsad, the English spy.

wind will take him where he must go. It will lead him to the end that is his. His name and Barsad's have been recorded.'

In the heat of the evening the people of Saint Antoine sat outside on door steps, in windows, on dirty street corners for a breath of air. Madame Defarge, her knitting in her hand, went from group to group of knitting women.

Her husband watched her from his door. 'A strong woman!' he said to himself, 'A fine woman!' and as darkness closed slowly around him he listened to the drums of the Royal Guard beating far away.

Just as surely, another darkness was closing around Saint Antoine and the whole of France. Soon the same women would sit knitting as they counted dropping heads.

CHAPTER EIGHTEEN

The Night

Never was the sunset more beautiful than on that night. In the quiet garden in Soho, the Doctor and his daughter sat watching the pale moon rising in the last dying glow of day. Lucie was to be married tomorrow.

'I am so happy, my dear father,' said Lucie. 'But I want you to know that if I had never seen Charles, I would have been happy with you. Are you happy, my dear father?'

'Yes, my darling. My future is far brighter, Lucie, seen through your marriage, through your happiness with Charles.'

She kissed him, then laid her head on his shoulder.

'See,' said the Doctor, raising his hand towards the moon. 'I used to look at her from my prison window. I could not bear to look at her shining on what I had lost.'

Lucie heard his words with a strange thrill. This was the first time her father had ever mentioned his years of suffering.

'I have looked at her thousands of times,' he went on, 'and

wondered whether your mother was still alive, whether you had even been born, whether you were alive.'

Lucie kissed his hand.

'You appeared in my dreams. You – my imaginary daughter or son – came to my cell in the Bastille.* You undid my chains, and took me away to freedom. And then,' he took her face in his hands, 'one day, that dream came true.' He kissed her and they held each other in silence for a long time before going inside.

CHAPTER NINETEEN

Nine Days

The sun shone brightly on the marriage morning, as the bride waited outside her father's room with Mr Lorry and Miss Pross (the only guests). Behind the closed doors, the Doctor was speaking with Charles Darnay.

'And so,' said Mr Lorry, moving around the bride to admire her, 'and so it was for this, my sweet Lucie, that I brought you across the Channel when you were a baby.'

He kissed her tenderly on the forehead and said, 'Now, Lucie, you must not worry. Miss Pross and I will take good care of your father while you are in Warwickshire. In a fortnight's time, when he comes to join you in Wales, he will be in the best of health.'

When the door of the Doctor's room opened, and he came out with Charles Darnay, the old man was as pale as death. However, acting quite normally, he gave his arm to his daughter and took her downstairs. Everyone got into the

* The Bastille is a castle on the edge of Paris, near Saint Antoine, built in the fourteenth century. Political prisoners were held there. It was destroyed by the French people in 1789.

carriage Mr Lorry had hired and soon, in a church nearby, Charles Darnay and Lucie Manette were happily married.

As soon as the young couple had left for their honeymoon, Mr Lorry noticed that a great change had come over the Doctor. Whey they got upstairs, the old man wandered away to his room.

'I think,' Mr Lorry whispered to Miss Pross, 'We had better not disturb him just now. I will . . .' He stopped speaking. Both of them had heard the low knocking sound.

'Oh dear!' cried Miss Pross. Mr Lorry said what he could to calm her and went into the Doctor's room. He found the old man bent busily over his shoemaker's bench.

'Doctor Manette! My dear friend, look at me!'

He looked up at Mr Lorry a moment, as if he were angry at being disturbed, then bent over his work again. For almost an hour, the banker spoke to the shoemaker but he did not reply.

'This must be kept secret from Lucie,' Mr Lorry said to Miss Pross later. 'I shall stay here tomorrow and watch over him.' That afternoon, Mr Lorry made arrangements to take time off work, for the first time in his life.

The next day, Mr Lorry sat in the shoemaker's room. Time and time again, Mr Lorry tried to make conversation with him, but the old man worked on in silence. Eventually he realized it was useless.

Mr Lorry's hope began to fade, and his heart grew heavier. The third day came and went, the fourth, the fifth. Six days, seven, eight. And with every hour the shoemaker's skill grew. Never had he concentrated so hard, never were his hands as expert as in the dusk of the ninth evening.

Watching him anxiously, Mr Lorry fell asleep in his chair.

It was the sun shining through the window that woke him the next morning. He got up stiffly, and was amazed to see that the bench and tools had been put away. Manette, in a clean suit, was sitting reading by the window. The Doctor looked up from his book and saw Mr Lorry staring at him. He smiled, clearly understanding his friend's shock.

'The shoemaker will never need his tools again,' he said.

'Did he die last night, while I was asleep?'

'Yes. He passed away.'

'Then we may destroy his tools, Doctor.'

Manette looked at his bench and tools and thought for some time. Finally, he said, 'Yes, Mr Lorry, we may.'

When the Doctor and the newly-married pair returned from Wales, the first person to visit them was Sydney Carton. Although Carton's physical condition had not improved, Charles Darnay noticed that he seemed friendlier than before.

Carton took Darnay to one side. 'Mr Darnay,' he said. 'I want us to be friends.'

'We already are, I hope.'

'Then you have forgotten a certain occasion when I was drunker than usual?'

'I have, yes.'

'I will never have any of the higher and better qualities of men, Mr Darnay. I am a dog who has never done any good and never will.'

Darnay saw the hopelessness in Carton's eyes. 'I don't believe you "never will",' he said, not really believing his own words.

'Thank you, Charles,' Carton said sincerely, and he left.

That night, in their bedroom, Lucie said to her husband, 'Charles, I think Mr Carton deserves more respect than you have for him.'

'Why is that?'

'I – I know he does. Try to forget his faults. He has a heart he very rarely shows. It is his heart that is deeply wounded. I have seen it bleeding.' She took him by the hands. 'I am sure that he is capable of good things, even great things.'

CHAPTER TWENTY

Echoing Footsteps

Time passed, happy times, and soon the echoes of a baby's tiny feet could be heard in the peaceful garden. But as Lucie sat watching her daughter's first steps, she sometimes felt afraid – as very happy people often do – that their happiness might end one day.

Years passed, and her husband's strong and successful footsteps, and her father's firm and equal footsteps echoed in the garden. And as those years passed, Sydney Carton visited from time to time. Lucie saw how her daughter had a strange sympathy for him. Carton was the first stranger to whom she ever held out her little hand.

She also heard the echoes of her admirer Mr Stryver pushing his way up the legal ladder, dragging his useful Jackal behind him. Stryver was rich, and had married a widow with property.

But there were other echoes. Their sounds could be heard faintly in the distance all through this time, and on little Lucie's sixth birthday those sounds began to grow much louder. They were the sounds of a great storm rising in France.

One hot wild night in the middle of July 1789, Mr Lorry came in late from Tellson's and sat down by the window with Lucie and her husband.

'We have been so busy all day!' said the exhausted banker, nervously pushing back his little brown wig. 'I have never known a time like this! All our customers in Paris are sending their money to England. Nobody knows what the reason is.'

CHAPTER TWENTY-ONE

The Rising Sea

As they sat talking by the garden window, the footsteps of a huge, angry mass of people were ringing through the streets of Saint Antoine. Earlier that day, a forest of naked arms had reached up to grab **weapons** handed down to them by Defarge and his companions. Guns, iron bars, knives, digging tools, **axes**, flashed over the heads of the feverish crowd. Now, there were thousands of Jacques, a roaring crowd of armed men and women, all of them thirsty for blood.

The centre of it all was the wine shop and Defarge, already dirty with gunpowder and sweat, was giving orders to his companions.

'You keep near to me, Jacques Three,' he said. 'And you, Jacques One and Two, separate from us and lead as many **patriots** as you can.'

Madame Defarge appeared, an axe in her hand, a knife and a gun in her belt.

'I see you are not knitting today, my wife!' said her husband.

'You shall see me at the head of the women.'

'Come, then!' cried Defarge. 'Patriots and friends, people of Saint Antoine, we are ready! To the Bastille!'

With a roar, the living sea rose. Their drums beating like thunder, wave after wave of them flowed towards the hated walls and towers of the Bastille prison.

A deep ditch, two bridges, huge stone walls, eight great towers, guns, fire, smoke. And in the fire and in the smoke the people of Saint Antoine fought for two fierce hours. One bridge was down!

'Fight, companions, fight!' shouted Defarge. 'Work, Jacques Two, Jacques One! Fight, Jacques One Thousand, Jacques Twenty Thousand! In the name of all the angels and devils, fight!'

'Follow me, women!' cried his wife. 'We can kill as well as men when
the Bastille is taken!'

'Follow me, women!' cried his wife. 'We can kill as well as men when the Bastille is taken!'

Guns, fire and smoke, but still the deep ditch, the single bridge, the huge stone walls, the eight great towers. With falling wounded, flashing weapons, burning buildings, screams, bravery, the living sea crashed against the hated walls for four fierce hours.

Then a white flag appeared and everyone roared one word: 'Surrender!' The sea flowed over the bridge, through the huge stone walls and in among the eight great towers.

The force of the sea was so great that many were crushed. Against a wall, hardly able to breathe, Defarge had his hands around a jailer's neck. 'What is the meaning of one hundred and five, North Tower!' he shouted. 'Tell me! Quick!'

'The meaning, monsieur? It is a **cell**, monsieur.'

'Kill him!' shouted Jacques Three.

'Show the cell to me!' shouted Defarge.

They went along dark corridors, climbed stairs that had never seen the light of day, passed damp, dirty cages where hundreds had died in chains. Once, they were inside the thick walls of the North Tower, they could not hear even the faintest sound from outside. At last, the jailer stopped in front of the low iron door of cell 105.

Almost an hour later, the three men came outside again. The sea had lost none of its force and the blood-stained crowd roared 'Defarge!' when its leader appeared.

They were holding the chief officer of the Bastille, an old man, who was trembling in his grey coat.

'See this, Defarge!' shouted his wife, standing next to the prisoner. She put her foot on the man's neck, raised her axe and cut off his head.

The crowd was wild with the taste of blood. They had at last got their revenge for the miserable years with no food or clothing under the iron hand of the aristocrats. In a great wave, the human sea flowed out of the prison and away into the city itself.

CHAPTER TWENTY-TWO

The Law of the Lamp

Madame Defarge, her arms folded, sat in the morning light and heat, watching the people in the wine shop and in the street. These people, who had known only hard and bitter bread, had now been tasting blood for a week. The short fat wife of a starved grocer sat knitting beside her. During the events of that last week, this woman had earned the name of 'The **Vengeance**'.

Defarge rushed into the wine shop and pulled off his red cap.

'Everybody remembers Foulon, don't they!' he shouted.

'Yes!' everyone cried.

'The man who told the people that if they were hungry they could eat grass!' shouted The Vengeance.

'Well he has been found − hiding in the country!' said Defarge. 'Some patriots have brought him to Paris.'

The Vengeance took her drum from behind the counter, Madame Defarge put her knife inside her belt.

'Patriots,' cried Defarge, 'Are we ready?'

People came pouring out of houses to join the crowd as it made its way to the town hall, dancing and shouting to the beat of The Vengeance's drum.

'Give us the blood of Foulon! Give us the head of Foulon! Give us the heart of Foulon! Give us the body and soul of Foulon! Tear Foulon to pieces, dig him into the ground so that grass may grow from him!'

Soon, the luckiest were packed inside the town hall. Thousands waited outside and in the surrounding streets. Inside, the Defarges, The Vengeance, and Jacques Three sat together in the front row, near the wicked old aristocrat.

'Tie a bunch of grass on his back!' cried Madame Defarge, pointing at him with her knife. 'Let him eat now!'

Three hours later, a man who had climbed the wall to see inside, shouted, 'They're bringing him out to the lamp!'

Defarge and Jacques Three dragged Foulon outside into the crowd. Hundreds of hands threw grass at the bruised and bleeding aristocrat as he was pulled to a street corner.

As her husband was preparing the rope, Madame Defarge let go of Foulon, as a cat might do with a half-dead mouse. She watched him begging for mercy, she watched the rope being put round his neck, she watched him dance as they pulled him up to hang from the lamp. And with his mouth full of grass, and his head on the end of a long stick, the aristocrat danced that night with the common people.

It was almost morning when the last customers left Defarge's wine shop, and as he closed the door, he said to his wife, 'At last it has come, my dear!'

'Almost,' was her reply.

CHAPTER TWENTY-THREE

Fire Rises

Alone in the midday heat, the road-mender worked in the dust from which he came and to which he would one day return. Around him lay a ruined country, squeezed dry by the aristocracy. Every miserable leaf, every yellow blade of grass, every village, animal, fence, house, the earth they stood on, everything was like his aching body – broken and worn out.

He looked up from his work and saw a long-haired, wild-looking stranger approaching on foot. He sat down on a heap of stones and waited for the ghostly-looking figure to arrive.

'How goes it, Jacques?' said the man in a Parisian accent.

'All is well, Jacques,' the road-mender replied. The weather-beaten Parisian looked down into the valley below, took out his pipe, filled it and lit it. His feet were bleeding in clumsy wooden shoes filled with leaves and grass.

'Tonight?' said the road-mender.

The exhausted traveller lay down on the heap of stones.

'What time do you finish work?' he asked.

'At sunset.'

'Wake me then.'

Towards the end of the long afternoon, during a short storm, the road-mender stopped working and watched the rain running down the sleeping man's face. When the sun was low in the west and the sky glowing, he woke the stranger from the city.

The man got up, scratched his beard and adjusted his dusty red night cap. His cracked lips opened into a toothless smile and, without a word, he walked off through the fields.

That night, after their poor supper, the villagers did not go to bed. They gathered around the fountain in the dark, whispering, waiting, looking in the direction of the château.

Gabelle, the Marquis's tax-collector and farm manager, watched this unusual behaviour from his window. Growing increasingly worried, he went up onto his roof. He stared at the distant château, only just visible in the darkness. Then he saw the huge building begin to glow with a strange light from within. Soon he could see flames shooting out of twenty or more windows.

'Fire!' he shouted. 'Help! the château is on fire!'

But the road-mender and his two hundred and fifty friends ignored the cries. They stood with folded arms watching the great column of fire rise in the sky.

Châteaux were burning and tax-collectors were hanging from lampposts all over France, as Gabelle ran downstairs to lock himself inside his house. However, that night, as he sat on his roof, shaking with terror, he had no idea how lucky he was.

CHAPTER TWENTY-FOUR

Pulled into the Storm

For three years the Revolution had blown over France like a red-hot wind, and Tellson's Bank in London had become a meeting place for French aristocrats who had escaped to England.

On a misty day in August 1792, Tellson's was, as always, crowded with complaining Frenchmen as Mr Jarvis Lorry sat talking with Charles Darnay.

'I agree. I am not getting any younger,' said the seventy-seven-year-old banker, 'But the truth is, my dear Charles, that I have no choice. I *have* to go. We must save the important records and papers in our Paris office.'

'But the city is too dangerous!' Darnay replied.

'For a harmless old man like me? Nonsense! Besides, I am taking Jerry with me as a bodyguard.'

'You are a brave – and stupid – old man,' said Darnay. 'I wish I were going myself,' he added restlessly, thinking aloud.

A clerk came over and gave an envelope to Mr Lorry. Translating, Mr Lorry read aloud, 'Urgent. To Monsieur the Marquis of Evrémonde, care of Tellson's Bank, London.'

Darnay's heart suddenly began to beat very fast.

He had told Doctor Manette his real name on his marriage morning. The Doctor had promised to keep the secret. Not even Lucie knew, so how could Mr Lorry? The answer, he soon realized, was that Mr Lorry didn't.

'I have made inquiries,' said the clerk. 'Nobody knows him.'

'A mistake, probably,' said Mr Lorry. 'I will take it back to Paris with me.'

'No, don't,' Darnay said. 'I know him. I know where he lives. I can deliver it for you if you want.' He put the letter in his pocket. 'When are you leaving for Paris, Mr Lorry?'

'I shall be leaving directly from here, tonight at eight.'

'When I have delivered this, I shall come back and see you off.'

Darnay left the bank immediately, went round the corner and opened the letter. This is what he read:

> *Prison of the Abbaye,*
> *Paris.*
> *21 June 1792*

> *Monsieur the Marquis,*
> *My house and yours were burnt to the ground. The villagers brought me to Paris and I was thrown into this prison. My crime, they tell me, is 'Treason against the people', and without your generous help, I will lose my head for it. I have tried to tell them that I have worked – on your instructions – for the people, and not against them. I have told them that it was you who instructed me to collect no rent or taxes from the villagers during these last years. But they tell me my crime is to have worked for an **emigrant** aristocrat. Monseigneur, please hear my cry for help! Please, save me from this house of horror!*

> *Your faithful servant,*
> *Gabelle.*

It did not take long for Darnay to make up his mind. He would go to Paris and save the servant whose only crime was to have been faithful to him.

Late that night of the 14 August, after he had said goodbye to Mr Lorry, he wrote two letters: one to Lucie, explaining why he had to go to Paris, telling her he would not be in danger; the other to the Doctor, asking him to take good care of his wife and daughter. He got onto his horse shortly before midnight and rode away, an invisible force pulling him into the heart of the storm.

CHAPTER TWENTY-FIVE

The Emigrant

Crossing France in the autumn of 1792 was a slow business. Every town and village had its group of armed citizen-patriots who stopped the traveller, questioned him, inspected his papers, looked for his name in lists, turned him back or sent him on, or stopped him and took him prisoner. All this was done in the name of the Indivisible Republic of **Liberty**, Equality, **Fraternity**, or Death.

Exhausted by yet another day of delays – he had been stopped twenty times along the road – Darnay went to bed in an inn in a small town in northern France, still a long way from Paris.

He was woken in the early hours of the morning by a worried official and three ragged patriots in red caps. The redcaps, armed and smoking pipes, sat down on his bed.

'Emigrant,' said the nervous official, 'I must send you on to Paris with these three men. You will travel much quicker with them, and they will protect you.'

'I would certainly be happy to travel faster than I have done so far,' said Darnay, 'but do I need protection?'

'Silence, aristocrat!' said one of the patriots. 'You must have protection – and you will pay for it.'

'I see I have no choice,' said Darnay.

'Choice! Listen to him!' said the same redcap. 'We are doing you a favour, aristocrat!'

He got dressed, paid them the large sum they demanded, and they set off, travelling all night in the driving rain. By evening the next day they had reached the town of Beauvais. A threatening crowd gathered to watch them get off their horses, and several people shouted, 'Down with the emigrant!' Darnay decided to stay on his horse.

'Emigrant, my friends?' he replied, shocked. 'But you see me here in France?'

A large man pushed his way forward. 'Dirty emigrant!'

The innkeeper stood in his way. 'Let him be!' he said, trying to calm the man. 'He will be judged in Paris.'

'Yes!' shouted the man to all around. 'Judged as a traitor!'

The crowd, roaring their agreement, moved closer.

Seeing the danger to his customer, the innkeeper pulled Darnay's horse quickly into the **courtyard** of the inn. The three redcaps, one of whom was drunk, followed.

'Friends, you are wrong,' Darnay shouted back at the crowd. 'I am not a traitor.'

'You will be when the new law is passed!' shouted the man as the doors were closed.

'You may have saved me from the lamppost,' Darnay said to the innkeeper. Outside, the crowd were still shouting insults.

'What is this "new law" he spoke of?' Darnay asked.

'There is already a new law that the property of all emigrants must be sold.'

'I've never heard of this law. When was it passed?'

'On the fourteenth of August.'

'The day I left England . . .'

'Everybody says another law will be passed soon; declaring all emigrants to be traitors. The punishment will be death.'

They rested until the middle of the night, then left while the town was sleeping. When daylight came, they had reached the walls of Paris. The Barrier was closed and strongly guarded when they rode up to it.

'The prisoner's papers,' demanded the man in charge. Shocked by the use of the word 'prisoner', Darnay said that he was a free French citizen travelling with citizens he had paid to protect him.

'Where are the papers of the prisoner?' the man repeated. The drunk patriot had them in his cap, and produced them.

The man was very surprised when he read Gabelle's letter. He studied Darnay's face closely, then went inside. After a long wait he came out again and ordered the Barrier to be opened. The redcaps turned back towards the country, taking Darnay's horse with them. Alone, Darnay walked through the Barrier and followed the man into a very dirty guardhouse where soldiers lay around, either drunk or asleep. He was taken to an officer sitting at a desk.

'Citizen Defarge,' the officer said to the man, 'Is this the emigrant Evrémonde?'

'This is he.'

'Evrémonde, you are to be put into the prison of La Force.'

'Under what law?' cried Darnay, 'And for what crime?'

'We have new laws, Evrémonde,' the officer said with a hard smile, 'And new crimes, since you were last here.'

He wrote a letter and gave it to Defarge with the words: 'In secret.' Defarge told the prisoner to follow him, and they left with two armed guards.

As soon as they were outside, Defarge said, 'You married the daughter of Doctor Manette, once a prisoner in the Bastille. Your wife came to my house in Saint Antoine to take him away. Perhaps you have heard of me?'

'You are the owner of the wine shop!'

'Yes. In the name of the guillotine,* why did you come back to France!'

'You know the truth – you read the letter.'

'A bad truth for you,' Defarge said.

Sensing that perhaps Defarge had some slight sympathy for him, Darnay dared to ask him for help.

'Defarge, please could you do something for me? I must send a message to Mr Lorry of Tellson's Bank – he is the gentleman who came to your house with my wife. He is in Paris.'

'I will do nothing for you,' Defarge replied in a sad voice. I am the servant of the people. My duty is to the people.'

They walked on in silence, through narrow, dark and dirty

* The guillotine is a machine for cutting people's heads off. It was first used in France on the 25 April 1792.

streets. Within an hour, a jailer was leading Darnay along darker and dirtier corridors inside the prison of La Force.

'Yours,' the jailer said, showing him into a cold damp cell.

'Can I buy a pen, ink and paper?' Darnay asked him.

'You can ask that when you are visited. At present, you can buy your food and nothing more.'

CHAPTER TWENTY-SIX

The Grindstone

In Paris, Tellson's Bank rented part of a large house where, until recently, aristocrats had lived in luxury. The finely decorated rooms were now occupied by a group of violent, heavy-drinking patriots.

There was a look of horror on Mr Lorry's face that night as he looked out of the window. Outside in the courtyard stood the object of his horror: a grindstone, brought there by his noisy neighbours that morning.

'Thank God,' he said, 'that no one dear to me is in this city tonight! May He have mercy on all who are in danger.'

Less than a minute later, he turned white at the sight of the two figures who entered the room.

'What is this!' he cried, breathless and confused. 'Lucie! Doctor! What has happened? What has brought you here?'

'Charles is in Paris!' cried Lucie, pale with anxiety. 'He was stopped at the Barrier and sent to prison!'

Mr Lorry let out a cry. Almost at the same moment, the gates of the courtyard burst open and a noisy crowd poured in.

'Who are they?' asked the Doctor.

'Don't look!' cried Mr Lorry desperately. 'Doctor, don't go near the window!'

'My dear friend,' said the Doctor with a cool bold smile, 'there is not a patriot in this city who would hurt me, or my family and friends, knowing I was once a prisoner in the Bastille.'

Mr Lorry was not so sure and he hurried Lucie to his private rooms and locked her in. He rushed back and joined his friend by the window.

'He is in La Force,' the Doctor said quietly.

'La Force! God help him!' Mr Lorry said. He pulled the curtain back slightly and they watched the scene outside.

A group of about fifty people had come to sharpen their weapons. Their faces were lit up by the fire flying off the spinning grindstone. They were screaming like excited children, screaming like animals. Their wild faces, their axes, their knives, their clothes, their hair, their half-naked bodies were red with blood.

'They are murdering the prisoners,' said Mr Lorry. 'It may already be too late . . . Doctor, if you have the power you say you have, you can make these devils take you to La Force.'

Manette pressed Mr Lorry's hand and left the room.

Seconds later, the Doctor walked confidently into the crowd. Terrified, Mr Lorry watched him speaking to them until he saw arms raised and heard shouts: 'Long live the Bastille prisoner! Help for the Bastille prisoner's son-in-law in La Force! Save the prisoner Evrémonde in La Force!'

Mr Lorry watched them leave and went to Lucie. He found her with her daughter and Miss Pross. He told her that the people were taking the Doctor to see her husband.

Twice more during the night, crowds rushed in to sharpen their tools of death. Looking out of the window at dawn, Mr Lorry saw an exhausted murderer crawl into the owners' luxurious carriage and go to sleep.

For the time being the blood-stained stone stood still, but the great grindstone, Earth, continued to turn. Heavily, the day dragged on and in the early evening the Doctor still had not returned. Shortly after dark, Jerry Cruncher showed three visitors into Mr Lorry's office.

The Doctor walked confidently into the crowd and spoke to the people.
Terrified, Mr Lorry watched and heard shouts: 'Long live the Bastille
prisoner!'

'Defarge! Madame Defarge . . .' said Mr Lorry. 'It has
been years since I last saw you!' Stone-faced, they stood
there looking at him. Mr Lorry bowed to The Vengeance.
'Do you bring news of Doctor Manette?' he asked Defarge.

Without a word, Defarge handed him a piece of paper. Mr
Lorry read the message, in the Doctor's handwriting:

> *'Charles is safe, but I cannot leave La Force yet.*
> *Let Defarge see Lucie.'*

'Come with me, Defarge,' said Mr Lorry, joyfully relieved,
'Madame Defarge and your friend can wait here.'

'Madame comes with us,' said Defarge mechanically. 'To
recognize their faces and know them. It is for their safety.'

They found Lucie crying, alone. Defarge gave her a note.
She read it aloud:

> *'Dearest, take courage. I am well, and your*
> *father has influence here. You cannot reply to*
> *this. Kiss our child for me.'*

Lucie was so overcome with joy she kissed Madame Defarge's hand. She pulled her hand away from Lucie's lips and
continued knitting. Lucie looked up and, meeting the
woman's cold stare, she felt suddenly afraid. Mr Lorry saw
this.

'My dear,' he explained, 'I believe Madame Defarge wishes
to see those whom she has the power to protect. Is that not
so, madame?'

'Is that his child?' said Madame Defarge, pointing a knitting
needle at little Lucie.

'Yes, madame,' answered Mr Lorry. 'Their only child.'

Madame Defarge turned to her husband. 'I have seen
them,' she said. 'We may go now.'

Lucie laid her hand on Madame Defarge's dress. 'As a wife

and a mother, I beg you to have pity on me. Tell me you will do my husband no harm.'

Madame Defarge turned to her friend The Vengeance. 'All our lives we have seen wives and mothers suffer, from poverty, hunger, thirst, sickness. Does she think her troubles bother *us*?' She turned and went out, The Vengeance following. Defarge went last, and shut the door quietly.

'That woman seems to throw a shadow on me and on all my hopes,' Lucie said.

'A shadow! Not at all!' said Mr Lorry, secretly greatly troubled. 'Courage! So far all goes well for us – much, much better than it has gone for many poor souls.'

CHAPTER TWENTY-SEVEN

Fifteen Months

Manette did not return until three days later.

He came back hollow-eyed, as pale as death. He had seen scenes of indescribable horror. During those four days and nights, eleven hundred defenceless prisoners, men, women and children, had been killed by the people. Neither he nor Mr Lorry told Lucie anything of what had happened – she only knew that the political prisoners were in danger.

He described to Mr Lorry the so-called 'court' inside the prison, where self-appointed judges – Defarge was one of them – sent people to their deaths. They had no proper trial or **execution**, they were simply taken outside and thrown to the people. Everywhere, rats were feeding on their bodies.

In that Hall of Blood called a court, the ex-prisoner of the Bastille had begged for his son-in-law's life to be spared. And he had succeeded. But as they were about to release him, for some reason they changed their minds: he must stay in prison.

However, in spite of the horrors he had seen, and in spite

of Charles's still extremely dangerous situation, the Doctor was full of hope. He had returned a completely changed man, with newly-found inner strength and confidence.

'My dear friend,' he said to Mr Lorry, 'I see now that my years of suffering were not just waste and ruin. It was all towards a good end. I *know* that I can save Charles – as Lucie saved me! All we need is time.'

But time had already been swept away by events, events that nobody could control. Suddenly, a new age had begun, an age of Liberty, of Equality, of Fraternity; and in this great new Revolutionary Age, the days flew by as though in a wild dream.

It was a dream of blood and terror, a dream in which a terrible, blood-thirsty machine cut off the heads of the innocent, of the guilty, of a king, of a queen, of a ruling class; it was a dream in which the streets and rivers were full of the rotting bodies of the murdered; it was a dream in which the emigrant Charles Evrémonde lay in his cell for a year and three months without trial.

During those fifteen months, the Doctor never gave up hope. He was now a well-known and respected man in Paris, and continually used what influence he had to protect Darnay. Also, he used his skill as a doctor, working day and night to save the sick – rich and poor alike. He had asked to be appointed Doctor of the prisons, and was now able to see Darnay from time to time.

On a snowy day in December, the never-tiring Doctor hurried into the empty courtyard of the Bank. He was returning from a visit to La Force, and Lucie rushed out to meet him.

'His trial is fixed for tomorrow,' he said, breathless. 'He doesn't know yet – I've just been given the information. He will be moved to the Conciergerie prison where the trial will take place. I have made arrangements for his papers to be . . .' He stopped, turned around, and instantly hid Lucie's eyes from the sight.

One. Two. Three. Three death carts went past, full of prisoners. The crowd were shouting cruel jokes:

'It's your turn to kiss the National Razor, the razor that shaves shorter than any other!'

'It's the best cure for a headache known to Man!'

'Soon you will kneel down beneath her, sneeze, and find your head in a basket!'

CHAPTER TWENTY-EIGHT

Liberty

Every evening, the Tribunal* sent out a new list of names to each of the prisons.

In the great hall of La Force that night, the prison officer smiled as he read out the first of the twenty-three names in the 'Evening Paper' (as the jailers jokingly called it).

'Charles Evrémonde, called Darnay!'

Darnay stepped forward, knowing they were his first steps towards almost certain death the next day. Prisoners around him whispered hurried words of kindness. Out of the other twenty-two names called, only nineteen were recorded as present: one had died in prison and been forgotten, and two others had gone to the guillotine long ago.

The journey to the Conciergerie was short and dark. The night Darnay spent in one of its rat-filled cells was long and cold. The next day, fifteen people were taken to the Tribunal before he was. All fifteen were sentenced to death and their trials took a total of an hour and a half.

'Charles Evrémonde, called Darnay.'

Standing in front of the Five Judges, Darnay looked around the audience. Most of the men in the noisy, disorderly

* A tribunal is a type/form of law court, in this case with five judges.

crowd were armed. So were many of the women. People were laughing, shouting, eating, drinking. He recognized Defarge, whom he had not seen since his arrival at the Barrier. He was sitting at the front with a woman who was knitting. Unlike the others they spoke to each other quietly, secretively.

He spotted his father-in-law. The old man gave him a brave, encouraging smile. Time after time, during his visits to La Force, they had practised what he had to say at the trial.

'Charles Evrémonde, called Darnay,' said the Public Prosecutor.* 'You are accused of being an emigrant, and therefore an enemy of the Republic. Under the new law, the punishment is death.'

'Enemy of the Republic! Take off his head!' people shouted.

Darnay replied by saying he had given up his riches and his aristocratic life to go and live in England from his own work. He had preferred to do this rather than live from the work of the poor people of France.

Did he have any proof of this?

Yes. As witnesses he had Alexandre Manette and Lucien Gabelle.

Cries of praise for the well-known good Doctor, friend of the Republic, rose up in the audience. Eyes that had looked murderously at Darnay moments before were now seeing him in a slightly different light.

And in England, he had married Alexandre Manette's daughter?

Yes.

Why did he come back to France when he did?

He had come back to save the life of citizen Lucien Gabelle. Was that a crime in the eyes of the Republic?

'No!' the people cried enthusiastically.

Did he have any proof of this?

Yes, there was Gabelle's letter, which had been taken from

* A public prosecutor is the same as an attorney-general.

67

him at the Barrier. (He knew the Doctor had made sure it would be among the papers given to the Five Judges.)

The letter was read out. There were murmurs of approval.

When Doctor Manette, hero of the Republic, was questioned, his clear answers made a great impression. He showed that Darnay was his first friend after his release from the Bastille; that Darnay had been accused by the aristocratic English Government of being a traitor and a friend of the United States. This brought more shouts of approval and as he went on he won more and more sympathy for the prisoner. Soon everybody in the court was on the emigrant's side. Before the Doctor had finished, the jury declared that they had heard enough.

There were roars of approval as the jury announced their votes. Every one was in Darnay's favour and he was declared free. People who had previously screamed for his blood were now shaking the emigrant's hand, slapping him on the back, with tears in their eyes.

Outside, Darnay and Manette were lifted onto the shoulders of celebrating men and, in the middle of a sea of dancing and singing redcaps, they were carried home.

When they entered the courtyard of the Bank, Lucie ran out and threw herself into Darnay's arms. As he held her and kissed her, his tears mixing with hers, the crowd danced faster and faster around them. They raised a young woman up on their shoulders, calling her the Goddess of Liberty. With fire in her eyes, she shook her blood-stained sword in the air, shouting, 'Liberty, Equality, Fraternity, or Death!'

CHAPTER TWENTY-NINE

A Knock at the Door

The Goddess of Liberty led her People away into the streets.

The re-united couple knelt down and prayed, thanking·

God for their happiness. Then, taking Lucie in his arms again, Charles said, 'Go and speak to your father now. No other man in France could have done what he has done for me.'

She went to him and laid his head on her breast, as she had done once long, long ago.

'Don't tremble, my darling,' he said. 'He is safe now. I have saved him.'

Holding him closer to her, she looked up at the darkening winter sky, knowing that at that very moment carts full of innocent people like Charles were rolling through the streets. A sudden, unknown fear came over her, as heavy as the thick dark air around her.

Miss Pross, crying with emotion, noticed how pale Lucie's face had suddenly become. 'There's nothing more to worry about now, my Ladybird,' she said cheerfully. 'We'll soon be safely back in England. "Never give up, hold up your head and fight," is what my dear fine wonderful brother Solomon used to say, God save his kind sweet soul – wherever he is.'

Lucie watched Miss Pross and Jerry hurrying out of the courtyard, going to buy food for the journey. They were all leaving tomorrow, leaving a city full of fear, distrust and revenge. Later, she, her husband, her father, and her child sat united again by the bright fire. She watched as the old man told his granddaughter the story of a great and powerful fairy who opened a prison wall and let out a prince.

'What was that?' Lucie said, suddenly afraid again. 'I heard something . . .'

'Now, now. It was nothing, my daughter,' said the Doctor, calming her. 'Our troubles are over.'

As he said these last words, there was a loud knock on the door.

CHAPTER THIRTY

Solomon

Miss Pross and Jerry crossed the Pont-Neuf bridge. When they had bought food, they went in search of the wine they needed. They avoided noisy wine shops full of redcaps, and eventually found a quieter one not far from the Tuileries Palace. It was full of smoke and workmen playing cards.

As their wine was being poured, a man got up to leave in a hurry and, in doing so, had to pass Miss Pross. When she saw him, she let out a scream. The wine shop was suddenly silent.

'What is the matter?' said the man quickly and quietly in English.

'Solomon! Oh my dear brother Solomon! After not seeing you and not hearing from you for so many years, I find you here!'

'Hold your tongue!' said the man nervously. 'If you want to speak to me, pay and we'll go outside.'

He looked suspiciously at Jerry Cruncher. 'Who's he?'

Jerry was staring at Solomon as though he had seen a ghost.

'Mr Cruncher,' replied Miss Pross who had burst into tears.

Sweating now, Solomon turned to the audience and gave a few words of explanation in French. Everyone began talking again and they went outside.

'Don't expect me to be surprised to see you,' he said. 'I knew you were in Paris. It is my job to know who is here and who is not here. I am – an official.'

Jerry Cruncher touched Solomon on the shoulder. 'I know you,' he said. 'I've seen you somewhere before.'

'Correct, Jerry,' said a voice behind them. They looked round. Sydney Carton smiled at them and bowed to Miss Pross.

'I arrived at Mr Lorry's house yesterday, Miss Pross, while you and Lucie were out. Mr Lorry and I thought I had better remain . . . absent until all was well.'

Miss Pross was still too shocked to say anything. Jerry was staring at Solomon again, scratching his head.

'Yes, Jerry,' said Carton with a sigh, 'You saw this man at the Old Bailey, shortly before his death. As you can see, he has been resurrected.'

Jerry suddenly remembered the face . . . and a night in a cemetery several years before. 'The coffin full of stones . . .' he whispered to himself, staring at Barsad. 'The dead spy . . .' he said out loud. Barsad's snake-like eyes met his.

'Miss Pross,' said Carton, seeing that she was beginning to understand. 'Your brother and I have some urgent business to talk about. You will be able to see him later, no doubt. Jerry will take you home to the Bank now. I am absolutely sure you are very much needed there.'

'Solomon!' cried Miss Pross. 'Promise you'll come and see me!'

The spy said nothing.

'Solomon!'

Jerry led her away.

It was Mr Lorry who told them when they arrived back at the Bank that Charles had been arrested again. He was accused of crimes his family committed years ago. They had taken him to the Conciergerie. He would be judged again to-morrow.

CHAPTER THIRTY-ONE

A Winning Card

An hour before he had met Miss Pross and Jerry, Carton had seen Barsad coming out of the Conciergerie prison. He had followed the spy to the wine shop, sat at a table near him, and listened to his conversation with another familiar face from the Old Bailey: John Cly.

Barsad was now working for the new Republic, as a spy in the prisons, and Carton heard almost immediately – to his horror – that Charles had been arrested again. He was still listening, hoping to hear information that might help Charles, when Miss Pross and Jerry walked in.

As soon as Jerry and Miss Pross had left for the Bank, Carton said a few words to Barsad, took him by the arm, and led him into the wine shop. He ordered a glass of wine and they sat down.

'Yes, Barsad,' said Carton, picking up the cards on the table, 'these are difficult times, desperate times.' He smiled, played with the cards a moment. 'Yes, a man's life is not worth a penny in this city, especially the life of a spy.'

Barsad wiped sweat from his face and drank his wine. Carton immediately poured him more, leaving his own glass untouched.

'Nobody likes a spy, Barsad,' he said lazily. 'Especially a spy who once worked for the aristocratic English Government. And who also worked for the fallen French aristocracy – spying on the poor people of Saint Antoine.'

'Keep your voice down!' Barsad whispered, sick with fear.

Carton slapped a card face down on the table. 'That was my first card. I'm sure it is a winning card – a *guillotine* card, don't you think? Especially if that lady you were talking about just now – the terrible lady who has recorded your name in her knitted list . . .'

'All right!' said Barsad. 'What do you want from me?'

'Not very much,' Carton replied, giving Barsad a sweet look of contempt. 'If I understand correctly, you can go in and out of the Conciergerie whenever you choose.'

'I tell you it is impossible to escape from there.'

'Who said anything about escape?' Carton said, picking up his glass. He looked at it for a moment, poured the alcohol slowly into the fireplace, and got up. 'Yes, these are desperate times, Barsad.' He threw down the cards. 'People have to play desperate games. Think of the desperate game Doctor Manette will have to play tomorrow. He will try to save his son-in-law again. The poor tired old man will play to win. I, however, am going to play to lose. Come with me, Barsad,' he said. 'Let us finish our conversation elsewhere, in private.'

Carton returned to the Bank not long afterwards. Jerry told him Miss Pross and the Doctor were upstairs comforting Lucie. He found Mr Lorry alone, staring into the fire with tears in his eyes. The terrible shock of the second arrest had weakened him. He was a much older man now.

Carton told Mr Lorry that he had made an arrangement with Barsad. He would be able to see Charles in prison once after the trial if . . . if he was sentenced to death. If he was sentenced to death, he would be kept overnight before going to the guillotine the next day.

'Seeing a sentenced man will not save him,' said Mr Lorry.

'I never said it would,' Carton replied. 'Lucie must not be told about this. And I had better not see her. How does she look?'

'Anxious and unhappy, but very beautiful.'

'Ah!' It was a long, sad sound, like a sigh. 'And you have finished your work here, sir?' he said after a long silence.

'Yes, as I was telling you last night, the Bank no longer needs me here. I have my travelling papers. I was ready to go.'

They were both silent.

'You have a long life to look back on, sir,' said Carton, staring into the fire.

'I am in my seventy-eighth year.'

'You have been useful to others all your life, constantly occupied, trusted and respected.'

'I have been a man of business all my life, that is all.'

'Many people will miss you when you leave this world.'

'Nobody would cry for me, Mr Carton.'

'How can you say that! Wouldn't *she* weep for you? Wouldn't her child?'

'Yes. Yes, thank God. I didn't quite mean what I said.'

Carton turned his eyes to the fire again, and after a few moments' silence he said, 'I would like to ask you, does your childhood seem far away to you now?'

'Twenty years ago, yes, it did. But not now, not at this time in my life. The closer I get to the end the further I come round the circle, back to the beginning again. I remember events in my childhood now which I thought I had forgotten.'

'I understand the feeling!' said Carton, a sudden brightness in his eyes. He got up and put on his coat.

'You are going out?' Mr Lorry asked him.

'I feel restless. I feel like wandering about the streets tonight. Don't worry, I shall re-appear in the morning.' He bowed respectfully and left.

CHAPTER THIRTY-TWO

Night into Day

Sydney Carton had once been a student in Paris and he knew the city well. He easily found the street he remembered and the chemist was closing his dim little shop when he arrived at half past ten. The tiny twisted man read the piece of paper Carton handed him.

'Whew!' he whistled softly. 'For you, citizen?' He prepared two small packets. 'Be careful to keep them separate, citizen. You know what happens if you mix them, don't you?'

'Perfectly,' Carton replied. He paid and left.

'There is nothing more to do until tomorrow,' he said outside, looking up at the moon and the fast-sailing clouds. He sounded peaceful, satisfied, confident – like a tired traveller who got lost, has at last found his road again, and now sees its end. Perfectly calm, he walked the empty, silent streets until the night, with the moon and the stars, turned pale and died.

The day came coldly as he walked along the deserted river

bank. He sat down and watched the clear light of the rising sun dancing in the fast-flowing current and then – for the first time in many years – he fell asleep a happy man.

Mr Lorry had already left to go to the trial when he got back. He drank a little coffee, ate some bread, washed and changed, and then left for the Conciergerie.

The courtroom was already full when he arrived. He found a place, hidden at the back. Mr Lorry was there in the court, and the Doctor was there. She was there, sitting beside him.

There was a sudden silence as the Public Prosecutor got up to speak.

'Charles Evrémonde, called Darnay, released yesterday, re-accused and re-arrested yesterday. You are accused of being an enemy of the Republic, of being one of a family of aristocrats who committed evil crimes against the people. The punishment for this is death.'

The President asked the Public Prosecutor for the names of the three who had accused him.

'Ernest Defarge, wine-seller of Saint Antoine. Thérèse Defarge, his wife. And Alexandre Manette, doctor.'

A great roar went up in the court, and in the middle of it, Doctor Manette stood up, pale and trembling.

'President, I protest! This is false, a fraud! The accused is my daughter's husband! My daughter and her loved ones are dearer to me than my life! Who and where is the liar who says I accuse my son-in-law!'

'Silence, Citizen Manette. Nothing can be dearer to a good citizen than the Republic.'

People shouted their agreement. The Doctor sat down, his lips trembling. Lucie took his hand.

Defarge was questioned by the Public Prosecutor. He said he was Manette's servant when he was a boy, and told the story of the doctor's imprisonment and of his release.

'You did good work when the Bastille was taken, citizen?'

'I believe so,' Defarge replied flatly.

'You were one of the best patriots there!' The Vengeance shouted. The crowd roared their approval. The President rang his bell, but The Vengeance ignored it.

'Citizen Defarge, tell the Tribunal what you did in the Bastille that day.'

'I knew Manette had occupied cell One Hundred and Five, North Tower. I went to the cell, searched it very thoroughly, and found written papers hidden in the chimney.' He produced some papers from his pocket. 'I give these papers to the court.'

'Let them be read.'

In dead silence and stillness, the papers were read.

CHAPTER THIRTY-THREE

The Mark of the Cross

I, Alexandre Manette, write this in my cell in the Bastille in December 1767, after ten years in prison. I write in secret, with a rusty nail and a mixture of blood and dirt. I write this while I am still in possession of my mind. I write the truth.

One moonlight night in the third week of December 1757 (I think the date was the twenty-second), I was walking along a deserted part of the bank of the Seine when a carriage came past, driven very fast. It stopped and two men got out. They were about my age and extremely alike, most probably twins. One of them asked me if I was Doctor Manette. I said I was.

He asked me to get into the carriage, explaining that my skills were needed urgently. It was not a request but an order, and I noticed they were both armed. I could do nothing but accept, and got into the carriage in silence.

We passed the North Barrier, went along dark country roads, and eventually arrived at a lonely house. As soon as we got out, I heard screams. We entered the damp and rotten old building, and the screams got louder as we went up the stairs.

The patient was a twenty-year-old woman, of extraordinary beauty. She was suffering from a brain fever and she had been tied to the bed with scarves and handkerchiefs. I noticed that one of the handkerchiefs was decorated with the badge of an aristocratic family. In the centre of the badge, there was the letter E.

Holding her down, I looked into her wild eyes. She was screaming constantly, always repeating the same words in the same order: 'My husband! My father! My brother!' Then she would count up to twelve and say 'Ssshh!' before repeating the same over again.

'How long has this lasted?' I asked the older brother. (By 'older' I mean the one who spoke with the most authority.)

'Since this time last night,' he said.

He brought a case of medicines to me, and I made a mixture of several drugs. I managed to get her to swallow it, and as I sat with her I noticed the room had only temporary furniture in it; that a blanket had been nailed over the window. I also noticed that neither of the men showed the slightest pity for the poor woman.

She had another violent attack, during which I was afraid she might swallow her tongue. Eventually, when she was calmer again, the older man told me there was another patient.

Lying in a room in the roof, on some hay on the floor, was a handsome farm boy of not more than seventeen. He was holding his side. I kneeled down beside him and saw the terrible wound, made by a sword. He was dying.

'I am a doctor,' I said. 'Let me examine you.'

'No! Leave me alone!' he whispered.

I turned to the older brother, and saw him looking down with disgust at the poor boy. I asked how he had been wounded.

'This stupid common dog forced my brother to fight him.'

The boy's eyes moved slowly back to mine again. 'Doctor,' he whispered, 'these aristocrats are very proud, but we common dogs can be proud too, sometimes. They steal everything we have, starve us, kill us, but we have a little pride left, sometimes.'

The young woman's condition was hopeless . . . Until the very end she went on screaming the same words.

He listened to the woman's screams and cries. 'She – have you seen her, Doctor?' I nodded. 'She is my sister, Doctor. She was a good girl. She married a good young man.' He looked at the older man. 'All of us lived on his land. The other one is his brother, the worst of their race. They think they are superior beings!' The boy's eyes turned to the younger brother.

'My sister had been married only a few weeks when he saw her. He asked her husband to "lend" her to him. He refused! What did they do? They attached him to a cart and drove him like an animal, laughing, whipping him until he fell. It was just before midday . . . The clock of the village church struck twelve . . . and he died.'

The boy knew he was close to the end. Forcing back the gathering shadows of death, he raised himself slightly and pointed at the eldest brother. 'Marquis.' He put his finger into the blood of his wound and drew a cross in the air. 'I mark you and your evil race with this cross of blood.' His arm dropped, and with it he dropped, dead.

I returned to the young woman. Her condition was hopeless. I cared for her for almost a week before she finally went the way of her brother. Until the very end she went on screaming the same words.

The two brothers were not at all concerned by her horrible end. They were more concerned by the death of her brother. It was embarrassing for their noble family that one of them had fought with a common dog, especially a boy. When I went downstairs, both of them were waiting, impatient to ride away.

They told me to promise never to speak of the things I had seen. I looked at them with contempt, and did not reply. The older one threw a quantity of gold on the table. I did not touch it, and they looked at each other as I walked out.

Early the next morning, the gold was left outside my door in a box with my name on it. I felt it was my professional duty to write to the Minister, describing the nature of the two cases, and stating the circumstances, but I took great care not to mention any names. I had just completed the letter when I was told the wife of the

Marquis of Evrémonde had come to see me. I made the connection with the letter E immediately.

She was a young woman, beautiful, but of weak health. She wished to speak to me in private.

She had partly discovered the main facts of the cruel story, of her husband's share in it, and of my being called. Her reason for visiting me was that she hoped to be able to help the poor girl secretly.

I told her how she and her brother had died in the house. Greatly disturbed, she said that one day God would let loose his anger on her evil family. They had made so many suffer.

She knew the girl had a sister, the only person in the family still living. She asked me if I knew this sister, and where she lived. She wanted to help her if she could. I could tell her nothing for I knew nothing, not even the family name.

She was a good, kind lady, and not happy in her marriage. How could she be! She was constantly afraid of her cruel husband, and his brother distrusted and disliked her. When I helped her into her carriage there was a pretty young boy inside, two or three years old.

'For his sake, Doctor,' she said, tears in her eyes, 'for my dear little Charles's sake, I would do anything to try and mend the terrible wrongs my family has done.' She rode away with her son in her arms. Ernest Defarge, my servant, took my letter to the Minister, and I expected never to hear anything more of the ugly affair.

That night — it was the last night of the year — a man rang at my door and demanded to see me. He said there was an urgent case in the Rue St Honoré, and it would not take long. He had a coach waiting.

As soon as I had got into the coach my arms were held and my mouth was tied with a handkerchief. In a dark street, the coach stopped and the two brothers appeared. The Marquis took my letter from his pocket and burnt it in front of me. Then the carriage brought me here.

I do not know whether my wife is alive or dead.

Yes, I, Alexandre Manette, writing in the year 1767, say that

one day the mark of the cross will be fatal to them and every last
one of their evil race!

CHAPTER THIRTY-FOUR

Dusk

A roar rose up in the court after the final words were read. It was the roar of a crowd thirsting for blood, revenge! Madame Defarge smiled at The Vengeance.

'Save your son-in-law now, my Doctor!' she shouted. 'Save him!'

There were roars of approval as, one by one, the jurymen voted. After the last vote, the President stood up.

'Charles Evrémonde, aristocrat, enemy of the people, you are sentenced to death within twenty-four hours!'

It was as though Lucie had received a fatal blow. In the middle of the noise and movement of the emptying court, she stood with her arms stretched out towards her husband.

'If I may just touch him, kiss him just once! Oh good citizens, have pity on us!'

'Let her. For just a moment,' said Barsad, who was standing near the jailers.

She rushed forward into Darnay's arms.

'Goodbye, dear darling of my soul!' he said. 'We shall meet again, in a world of peace and rest.'

'My husband! No! One moment more!' Charles was tearing himself away from her. Crying, he took hold of the Doctor's thin hand and kissed it.

'I understand,' he said to his father-in-law.

As the jailers took him away, Lucie stood with her hands joined in prayer. When he had gone out of the prisoners' door, she fainted and fell to the floor.

Sydney Carton left his corner and came and picked her up.

He took her outside and laid her in a coach. Her father, Mr Lorry and Carton got in beside her, and they left.

When they arrived at the Bank, Carton took her inside and laid her on a bench. Little Lucie stood crying beside her.

'Oh Carton, oh Carton!' cried the child, throwing her arms around him. 'I know you will do something to help mamma, to save papa!'

He bent down and put her cheek to his face. Then he knelt down beside her unconscious mother and touched her face with his lips.

He went into the next room and turned suddenly to Mr Lorry and Doctor Manette who had followed him. 'Time is short, Doctor,' he said. 'You still have some influence. Try everything.'

'I will go,' said Manette, 'to the Public Prosecutor and the President straight away, and to others too.'

'I shall come back at nine and hear what you have done,' said Carton. 'Good luck!'

Mr Lorry followed Carton out into the courtyard.

'There is no hope,' whispered the banker.

'No. He will die,' said Carton, and he walked away.

CHAPTER THIRTY-FIVE

Darkness

Sydney Carton paused in the street outside. After some thought he set off in the direction of the Saint Antoine. In the court, Defarge had described himself as the owner of a wine shop. It would not be difficult to find it.

On the way, he had dinner in a restaurant and, for the first time in years, he did not drink alcohol with his food. He fell asleep afterwards, and woke up refreshed at seven o'clock.

The only customers in the wine shop were Jacques Three and

The Vengeance. They were in conversation with the Defarges when Carton walked in. He sat down deliberately clumsily and shouted for wine – in deliberately bad French. By this time Madame Defarge was staring at him very curiously indeed.

Defarge brought him wine. 'Good evening,' he said. 'You are English?'

'Yes! Good evening, citizen!' Carton said, pretending to be drunk. 'I drink to the Republic!'

Defarge went back to the others at the counter.

'I swear to you,' said Madame Defarge, 'the Englishman is exactly like Evrémonde!'

'Yes, my dear, very much alike,' said The Vengeance. 'And I bet you are looking forward to seeing Evrémonde die tomorrow, aren't you!'

'I will only be happy when they are all **exterminated**!'

'Extermination, yes! All of them!' said Jacques Three.

'No, my wife. One must know when to stop,' said Defarge, eyeing her uneasily.

'Stop!' she said contemptuously. 'Stopping is for the weak like you! There is still that wife of his, isn't there? And his child. They are Evrémondes, aren't they!'

'Yes, dear wife, but –'

'And that Doctor! I have observed his face. It is not the face of a true friend of the Republic.'

'Magnificent!' said The Vengeance, kissing her friend. 'The citizeness is an angel!'

'And now, my friends,' said Madame Defarge, her eyes bright with anger, 'I will tell you. I will tell you *why* I will never stop until every last one of them is dead.'

'No, my wife, please,' said Defarge, taking her by the hand. 'Let us bury the matter now.' She took no notice of him.

'I was brought up among the fishermen of the seashore but I never forgot! What did I never forget, eh? That the family of farmers that was so injured by the Evrémondes was *my* family! Yes! The wounded boy was my brother! His sister was my sister! They killed her husband, my father, my mother. They killed all of them! All except me!'

The Vengeance and Jacques Three looked at Defarge.

'Yes,' he said quietly. 'This is so.'

'You can tell wind and fire to stop!' Madame Defarge shouted at her husband, 'but don't tell me!'

Customers entered and the conversation ended. The drunk Englishman paid and left, and at nine o'clock precisely, he arrived at the Bank. Mr Lorry was pacing up and down with anxiety: Manette had not been seen since he left at four.

They waited, wondering what the Doctor's delay could mean. Was there hope? He returned after midnight. As soon as he entered the room they realized there was no hope at all.

'Where is my bench, where are my tools?' said the old man. 'I must finish those shoes I was working on!' He let them take his coat off, then let them lead him to a chair by the fire. He asked for his tools again then sank into silence.

Carton picked up some papers which had fallen out of the Doctor's coat. They were travelling papers. He had succeeded in getting travelling papers for everyone, including Carton.

'Thank God!' he murmured, and turned to Mr Lorry. 'Sir, you, Lucie, and the child – all of you – are in great danger here. Have horses ready tomorrow, so that we may leave for England at two o'clock in the afternoon.'

'It shall be done!' the banker replied, encouraged by the young man's firm manner. 'I knew we could depend on you, Sydney!'

Carton took him gently by the arm. 'Dear sir, for her sake, and the child's, please tell her that it was Charles's last wish that they should leave tomorrow.'

'I will.'

'Now, listen carefully. You must be ready, in your seats in the carriage, here in the courtyard, at two. There must be a seat for me and the moment I arrive, take me in and drive away, do you hear! You must do exactly as I say.'

'We will.'

He kissed Mr Lorry's hand and said goodbye. Before leaving he went over and gently touched the Doctor's head. Outside, in the dark courtyard, he remained for a few moments, looking up at the light in Lucie's window.

CHAPTER THIRTY-SIX

Fifty-Two

Fifty-two heads from the Conciergerie would roll the next day: the heads of people as different as a rich government minister, a poor servant girl, and Charles Darnay.

Before dark, Darnay had been allowed to buy a pen, paper, and a light, and he sat alone in his cell writing to Lucie. He told her that he had known nothing of his family's responsibility for her father's imprisonment; told her to take care of her father and their daughter; and assured her that one day they would all be together again in heaven.

He wrote to Doctor Manette, saying much the same, and asking him to take care of his widow and daughter. To Mr Lorry he wrote expressing his friendship and respect, and asked him to take care of his family's affairs. When he lay down on his bed, he thought he had finished with this world.

In his sleep, he was free and happy, back in the house in Soho with Lucie again. She told him it was all a dream, that he had never been away to Paris. He woke up in the grey of early morning, not knowing where he was or what had happened. Then he realized – it was the day of his death.

He felt strangely calm, and hoped he could meet his end bravely, but as the hours went slowly by, he had more and more difficulty in controlling his thoughts. Time dragged on, the clocks ringing out numbers he would never hear again, and as he walked up and down his cell, his mind kept returning to one thing, a thing he had never seen, the guillotine.

Eleven gone for ever, twelve gone for ever . . . he knew his final hour was three . . .

The clock had just struck one when he heard footsteps and someone, obviously drunk, singing in English. The footsteps stopped outside his door, and he heard another man whisper in English: 'Be quick!'

Then the singer said loudly, 'Jailer, I feel weak. I have drunk too much. I think I am going to faint.'

'You'll be all right, we'll come and fetch you in ten minutes,' the other replied, equally loudly.

'You may have to carry me!' shouted the singer.

There were loud laughs and seconds later Sydney Carton stood in the cell, smiling. Darnay could hardly believe his eyes.

'I bring an urgent request from her. I have no time to explain why, but you must simply do what she asks – take your boots off and put mine on, quickly now.'

'Carton, there is no such thing as escape from this place!'

'Who said anything about escape? Your boots – hurry now! *She* wants you to wear them!'

Darnay obeyed. When he had put the boots on, they exchanged coats, and hats.

'Give me that ribbon you tie your hair with,' said Carton.

'This is madness, Carton,' said Darnay, undoing it.

'Now,' said Carton, 'I want you to write something down.'

'Write what?'

'Sit down and write what I say!' Darnay sat down. 'First, write the date,' said Carton. His hand, holding a handkerchief, moved slowly up behind Darnay's head and, suddenly, he held the handkerchief over Darnay's mouth. Darnay struggled before falling unconscious over the table.

Minutes later, tying his hair with Darnay's ribbon, Carton smiled at Barsad and said in a loud voice, 'Be careful how you carry my drunken friend. Leave me now.'

'Hah! You will soon be leaving *us*, Evrémonde,' Barsad replied in an even louder voice. The other two jailers laughed as they picked up the unconscious Darnay and carried him out.

Carton felt a strange thrill when the door closed, the key turned, and he was left alone.

◆　　◆　　◆　　◆

'Follow me, Evrémonde.'

Carton followed the jailer along damp passages. A clock struck two as he entered a large, dark room.

Some of the fifty-two were standing, some were seated, some were crying, some were restless, most of them were silent and still, looking at the ground. A pale young woman got up when she saw Carton enter.

'Citizen Evrémonde,' she said, touching him with her cold hand. 'I am the servant girl you met in La Force.'

'True. I forget what you were accused of.'

'Plots. What plots I do not know.' The sad smile with which she said this brought tears to Carton's eyes. 'I am feeling a little weak and I need courage, citizen Evrémonde. May I hold your hand?' Her eyes looked up to his and she suddenly realized. She was astonished, horrified. 'Are you dying for him?' she whispered.

'Shssh! And his wife and child. Yes.'

'Oh you will let me hold your hand, brave stranger?'

'Yes, my poor sister,' whispered Carton, 'To the very end.'

◆　　◆　　◆　　◆

At that same moment, a coach was stopping at the Barrier. The travellers' papers were handed out, and examined by the guard. Alexandre Manette, doctor, French. Lucie, his daughter, French. Her child, English. Jarvis Lorry, banker, English. Sydney Carton, lawyer, English. The guard was amused when he was told that the sleeping lawyer was drunk.

'A foolish young man. He will soon wake up in the fresh air of the country,' said Mr Lorry, who had replied to all the previous questions.

The guard signed all the travelling papers.

'We can leave, citizen?' Mr Lorry asked.

'Your road is clear. A good journey!'

CHAPTER THIRTY-SEVEN

The Deaf and the Dead

The Vengeance, Jacques Three and Madame Defarge sat talking.

'I cannot trust my husband in this matter,' said Madame Defarge. 'He is a good Republican, but he has his weaknesses. He does not understand why the wife and child must be exterminated.' She smiled. 'She will be at home now, awaiting her husband's death. I think I shall go and see her.'

'Why go and see her now?'

'Why? Because we need proof if we are to accuse her publicly of being a traitor. She will be crying for him. And it is a crime to weep for an enemy of the Republic, is it not?'

'Oh, what a wonderful admirable woman you are, my beautiful!' cried The Vengeance and kissed her.

'We will come with you,' said Jacques Three.

'No, I will not be long. I shall meet you at the guillotine. Here, take my knitting and save my usual seat for me.'

'Be sure to arrive on time, my sweet,' said The Vengeance.

'I will be there to see Evrémonde's head fall.'

They watched her walk away. 'What a fine, moral, strong, fearless citizeness she is!' said The Vengeance.

As the pitiless citizeness made her way through the streets, Miss Pross and Jerry Cruncher were packing their things. They had arranged to catch a light carriage at three. They would catch the others up on the road to Calais. Jerry rushed out to buy the food for the journey, and Miss Pross looked at her watch. It was twenty past two. She must get ready at once.

Hurriedly, she washed her face, and when she reached for her towel she saw there was a woman standing in the room.

'The wife of Evrémonde, where is she?' said the woman coldly, her dark eyes watching every movement Miss Pross made.

Miss Pross did not understand French, and did not like the look of the woman. 'I know your intentions are evil, whoever you are,' she said.

Madame Defarge did not understand English. 'I wish to see her, you stupid pig-like woman.' She took a step forward, looking around her at the disorder everywhere, at the half-packed luggage. 'Where is she? Have they gone!' she shouted.

'Don't come any further!' shouted Miss Pross, standing in front of the door of Lucie's room.

'Let me look in there!' said Madame Defarge, coming forward. 'Or I will tear you to pieces, you fat cow!' She tried to push past but Miss Pross grabbed her round the waist.

There was a blinding flash, a deafening crash, and Miss Pross found herself standing alone in a cloud of smoke.

When the smoke cleared and she saw the Frenchwoman she understood. She had had a gun hidden in her belt. Her body lay lifeless in a spreading pool of blood.

Miss Pross screamed out for help. She could not hear her own voice . . . 'Help!' she screamed . . . but she could not hear anything at all . . . And she never did again.

CHAPTER THIRTY-EIGHT

The Footsteps Die Out Forever

Along the Paris streets, six death carts roll, carrying the day's wine to the guillotine.

Among the fifty-two, some observe the sights along their last road with a steady, expressionless stare, others still watch with interest the ways of life and men. Some, with their heads down, are sunk in silent sadness. Several close their eyes and try to gather their last thoughts. One man is so drunk with horror that he sings and tries to dance.

The people along the roadside are curious to know which one Evrémonde is. He is standing at the back of a cart, talking to a young servant girl who holds his hand. He shows no interest in the scene around him, only in the girl. Here and there in the long street of St Honoré, cries are heard against him:

'Down, Evrémonde!' shouts an excited man. 'To the guillotine all aristocrats! Down Evrémonde!' He turns to the man next to him. 'Which one is he?'

'There, at the back of the third cart,' replies Solomon Pross, or John Barsad, if you prefer.

'Down, Evrémonde!' the man continues. Evrémonde's face turns towards him. He sees the spy and their eyes meet for a moment.

The clocks ring out three as the carts arrive at the guillotine. In front of the terrible machine, seated in chairs, women are busily knitting, waiting for today's entertainment. The Vengeance is among them, looking about for her friend.

'Thérèse!' she cries. 'Who has seen Thérèse Defarge?'

'She's never missed a single time,' says one of the knitters. 'Shout louder, my dear.'

'Thérèse!' shouts The Vengeance. 'Thérèse!'

Louder, The Vengeance, louder. She will never hear you.

Carton holds the hand of the servant girl as they stand and wait for the guillotine.

Evrémonde gets out of the cart with the servant girl. He turns her back to the machine which is already at work. Holding his hands, she says, 'I think you were sent to me by heaven.'

'And you to me, dear child,' says Sydney Carton. 'Keep your eyes on me. Think of no other object.'

'I think only of you! Will they be quick?'

'They will be quick. Don't be afraid.'

They speak as if they were alone, eye to eye, voice to voice, hand to hand, heart to heart, two children of the Universal Mother.

'Brave and generous friend, your kind strong face gives me so much support. Is the moment come?'

'Yes, sweet child.'

She kisses his lips; they say goodbye, knowing they will see each other again soon. Her hand does not tremble as it leaves his. She goes – is gone. The knitting women count twenty-two.

As Carton saw the crowd push forward to see him die, like a great mass of water, he repeated a line from the Bible, 'I am the Resurrection, I am the Life, said the Lord.'

As he stared down into the blood-stained basket he thought, 'I do a far, far better thing than I have ever done. I go to a far, far better rest than I have ever known.'

Twenty-three.

People said that night, that when his head was held up, his face was the most peaceful they had ever seen.

EXERCISES

Vocabulary Work

Look back at the 'Dictionary Words' in this book. Write ten sentences with *two or more* of the words in each one, to show that you understand the meaning of each of them.

Comprehension

Chapters 1–9

1 Name each of these people.

  a This man was a passenger on the Dover mail and a message was brought to him.

  b This woman sat knitting in a wine shop in Paris.

  c This man was accused of being a traitor but escaped prison because another man looked very much like him.

  d This man was sometimes known as The Jackal.

Chapters 10–18

2 Answer these questions.

  a Why did the Marquis throw a gold coin to the crowd?

  b Darnay wanted to tell Doctor Manette something, but the doctor did not want to hear it. What was it?

  c What did Sydney Carton tell Lucie Manette that later proved to be true?

  d Madame Defarge had a strange but clever way of keeping records of what was happening. What was it?

Chapters 19–27

3 Are these sentences true (√) or not true (x)?

  a Lucie's young daughter had a strange sympathy for Sydney Carton.

b Charles Darnay decided to go back to Paris because of a letter from Stryver, the tax collector.

c Jarvis Lorry was put in La Force prison.

Chapters 28–38

4 Put these sentences into the right order.

a Sydney Carton went to a chemist's shop in Paris to buy something.

b The servant girl kissed Sydney Carton goodbye before she died.

c Miss Pross screamed for help, but she could not hear anything at all.

d Darnay wrote to Doctor Manette, asking him to take care of his widow and daughter.

Discussion

1 What do you know about the French Revolution? What do you think Dickens thought about it, now that you have read this book?

2 'I am not worth your tears,' Sydney Carton tells Lucie Manette. Now that you have read all of the story, do you agree? Why?/Why not?

Writing

1 Dickens is critical of both the common people and the aristocracy, in different ways. What are these ways? Do you think he has more sympathy for one side or the other? Give examples from the story to support your opinion. Write about 200 words.

2 Look at the picture on page 43. Write three or four sentences about each of the characters in this picture. Describe their clothes and bodies. What do the expressions on their faces tell us about them?

Review

1 a Which character in the book do you like the most? Why?

b Which character in the book do you like the least? Why?

2 Write a short review of the book (250 words) giving a brief outline of the story.